The King Cried Murder!

Welcome to Georgian-era Windsor Castle for
the first in a series of historical crime novels by
Britain's finest practitioner of the traditional
mystery.

Set in the same period as the film *The Madness
of King George*, a young Fanny Burney, not yet
the famous literary figure she is to become, is a
maid-in-waiting to the Queen. The life of the
entire castle is affected by the wanderings and
ravings of the deranged monarch, and Fanny
does the best she can to soothe her mistress in
the midst of her troubles.

Then the murders begin…
And in some strange way Fanny has a connection to them…

GWENDOLINE BUTLER

THE KING CRIED MURDER!

First published in Great Britain 2000 by CT Publishing, PO Box
5880, Edgbaston, Birmingham, B16 9BJ

3801

A CIP catalogue record for this book is
available from the British Library.

ISBN 1-902002-15-6   The King Cried Murder!

Book design and typography by DP Fact & Fiction

Printed and bound in Great Britain by Caledonian International
Book Manufacturing, Bishopbriggs, Glasgow.

to Lucilla

THE KING CRIED MURDER!

ONE

It was certainly fortunate that Dr Burney was not at home when the royal messenger came.

"So we go together," Fanny said to her maid. "And your name is the same as the Queen's: Charlotte."

And who gave the girl her name but Dr Burney himself as she was christened, for christened as an infant she had never been. It was a ceremony, like marriage, not much observed in the social circles Charlotte Minden had been born in. The name Minden was a gift from Dr Burney too, a favourite battle of his, 1759 being in the *annus mirabilis* of the Seven Years War.

When the royal letter arrived, Dr Burney might have thought again about sending his talented, treasured daughter off to become maid-in-waiting to Queen Charlotte, wife to King George III.

He was a royalist, yes, indeed, a strong and loyal one, but he knew, none better, that a young woman without a dowry needed either a husband or to earn her living. Fanny had written a celebrated novel but it had not made her rich.

Fanny had accepted with a sigh. "So we will go together, maid to the Queen and maid to Miss Fanny Burney. Perhaps it may be an omen that you have the same name as the Queen." Another sigh. Was she a royalist, willing to dip the knee to that poor, always pregnant Queen? Without putting it into words, she pitied the woman, nothing more than a child bearing machine who had (as the country felt as funds were requested) more than done her duty.

Charlotte Minden, tall, handsome and strong, plucked from the riverside slums of London because of her sweet singing voice. "Except I am always called Mindy."

"Straighten your bodice, Mindy." Mindy could be casual about certain ties and buttons. I must learn to call her Charlotte, court ways must grow upon us as my father advised.

"Yes, miss." Mindy drew her bodice together. "—I love you, Miss Fanny Burney, with a love you can know nothing about it from the way you have lived. Not as I would love a man, as I have loved a man, but strongly all the same."

In the first place it must be recognised that a castle may be a prison and a palace a place of restraint.

Fanny Burney knew this full well but the prison was one she had found it necessary to enter, because a young woman of style and education, even though she has written a celebrated novel, but without a dowry is obliged to find herself employment. She had wept before entering this particular prison but she had accepted her life. With some reservations.

But there were compensations: Queen Charlotte was only as demanding as the rigours of her position demanded, the King himself was sociable and friendly. Mad, sometimes. Given to chasing a maid round the castle walls to give her a hug, but otherwise not troublesome.

Within the castle lived so many souls it was hard to count them although the castle comptroller tried hard. So many servants, so many cooks, so many scullions, so many of diverse functions like the boy whose sole duty it was to open the kitchen windows. A boy had been appointed to do this in the time of Queen Anne and a successor was still doing it.

As well as the state rooms, beyond which were the royal apartments and the nurseries and school rooms for the royal brood, there was the library where a quiet dark librarian held sway, and the picture gallery with the Keeper of the King's Pictures.

And this was only inside: outside, where the great building (which was really many buildings of different ages from William the Norman onwards) stretched out its arms, with courtyards and terraces, towers and stables were horses, dogs, grooms, carriages and stable boys.

Further down the steep slope of the hill, there were the royal chapel and the barracks for the soldiers. There was the row of houses where the Poor Knights of Windsor, pensioned off soldiers, lived out their somewhat rakish lives, perpetually threatened with reform or expulsion.

So many souls. Not to mention a great family (for they were all related one way or another) of cats who kept down the even greater hordes of mice and rats. These too were incestuous and internecine.

That day in London, 1786, someone tried to kill the King, stab him to death, no less.

Hardly a mystery there, someone always wanted to kill a King. Two Kings had been murdered already in England: Edward the Second in a cellar and Charles the First by an executioner's axe.

But this would-be murderer was a woman.

"She rushed at me with a knife as I bent to greet her," said the King in an excited voice, "but she did not touch me, I am not hurt." He repeated this several times in his excitement, ending, as ever, "What, what."

A mad woman everyone said, off to Bedlam with her. "Do not hurt her," the King had said as she was dragged away. She had rushed at him, saying he smelt of Kingship. "She has not hurt me." But she would soon be trussed up

11

in a strait-jacket inside the mad house walls while the inhabitants screamed and wailed all around her and not able to hurt anyone.

"See," King George had said, "the knife is blunt. What, what."

But there was a knife loose in Windsor that no one knew of yet which was both sharp and dangerous. The knife that was that moment reposing in a box in a drawer in a house in one of the seedier parts of Windsor down by the river Thames. Every so often the knife was taken out of the box to be sharpened, and then put back to wait.

The buyer of the knife had purchased it, saying that it was bought to "kill a pig." But no pig's throat had that knife cut, nor would it. Except possibly, just possibly, by way of practice while in waiting.

"This being 'in waiting' is a mighty tiring business, miss," said Charlotte Minden as she helped her mistress dress. "Out of one gown and then into another. And then what do you do but help her Majesty into her drawers."

"Mindy, be quiet." But Charlotte Minden, tall and handsome, towering over her slight young mistress, was never hushed but always spoke her mind. —But always remember she is loyal, Dr Burney had said when he sent Charlotte off to Court with Fanny, very loyal is Charlotte. He called her Charlotte, sometimes Minden. "I never assist with Her Majesty's..." Fanny hesitated, "...with her under garments, Mrs Fisher, her bath woman, does that. I only come in with the hoop."

And a size that hoop must be, thought Charlotte Minden, how many children has the Queen? Fifteen or sixteen, and a waist to suit, an inch on the waist with each child, I'll be bound.

She slipped the dress over Fanny's head, a simple morning dress.

"I put on the hoop and then the dress and then give the fan, and then I am done. I go off while the Queen is powdered."

"And does she sneeze while she is powdered? I have heard she gives a mighty sneeze while her hair is powdered."

"I think just a little snuffle." Fanny could see Charlotte Minden's face in the looking glass as her own hair was dressed. Their eyes met.

"And shall you go out tonight when you are done with this putting the Queen in and out of her clothes? The play?"

Fanny could see her maid's face in her looking glass and Charlotte Minden could see out of the window.

"There goes Major Petty... drunk already. A black eye too. Fighting again, those poor Knights, what a lot. As rowdy and rousting as could be," she watched the Major's slow progress up the hill. "But he's been on the town all night, anyone can see that, he's hardly got his shirt in his trousers," she turned back to Fanny. "Well, shall you go to the play, then?"

"You need not come with me." Fanny knew that Charlotte Minden had her own friends, her own diversions in the town.

"I'll come."

—Look after Fanny, Dr Burney had said. She is not like other people; she lives in her imagination. She is timid. — Not so timid as you think, Dr Burney, not when she is in love.

"He is not a good man, miss."

"I am going to the play because I mean to write a play, Charlotte, and this can only be done by learning, by watching and listening." Fanny turned away from the looking glass. "A man has nothing to do with it."

The bell that was her call to the Queen sounded, and she left. "I will wear the dark cloak tonight when we go to

13

the play, the one with the hood."

You could hide behind a hood like that, shield your face from view while looking out at the world. But that was not her motive, Fanny told herself, rather that Windsor's theatre and the streets on the way were windswept and cold.

"He is not a good man, James Manston," muttered the maid as she went about the room, tidying it up. "Not good at all, but devilish easy to be loved," she attended to Miss Burney's breakfast tray which the manservant would remove. "It's the nose, I avow, if a man has a good nose he is bound to be a good lover." She had herself had a lover or two, although it was a chancy business if you did not want to end up with a family you could not account for.

The footman came in, willing to joke and flirt, but this morning Charlotte Minden scurried him out, she was in no mood for his jokes just now. He had a pleasant, country boy's face, he came from one of the royal farms near Slough, but he must learn when a woman fancied to be joked with and when not.

He gave her a grin and a slap before carrying out the breakfast tray. He had a look of the King, Farmer George, and there were plenty of royal bastards around. So it was said, by the cynical old Thames Waterman, her father. She could hear him now, patting her cheek as he wished her goodbye and good eating at the royal court. Look out for yourself, girl, he had said. Kings always shed their seed around, don't come back to Bermondsey with a royal bastard under your petticoat.

The wind blew through the corridors of the castle, it was cold in the antechamber to the Queen's apartments, cold in her drawing room, cold in the gallery leading to the terrace, and even colder on the terrace itself. Here, every day when it was fine, and even on some when it was not, the whole royal family paraded up and down so that the popu-

14

lace below could see them, the King waving and bowing and the Queen and princesses nodding politely.

Fanny shivered while she waited to join them; she sneezed and then coughed. There was a special Windsor smell in this anteroom which tickled her nose. The smell was compounded of beeswax from the polish on the furniture, a spicy smell from bowls of herbs and over it all a musty smell which seemed to hang about the curtains and even clothes of the King and Queen. Mrs Schellenbarter, the Keeper of the Robes senior to Fanny, frowned.

"You do not sneeze in the Queen's company, nor cough," she commanded in her strong German accent—all the Queen's ladies in waiting were German, had come with her from Germany when she married, Fanny being English was unusual. "You choke, you hold your noise, but sneeze, no."

The lady was always ailing, and constantly calling upon the services of Dr Seaton, a tall, thin, acidic medical man who treated everyone with almost too much politeness.

Fanny hated Mrs Schellenbarter, whom she had every reason to believe disliked her back. Fanny was young, pretty and English, she had written a novel, *Evelina*, which the King admired. All grounds enough for the older woman to find her tiresome company.

As Fanny held her nose to keep back the sneeze, (although the Queen was nowhere near and anyway often gave tremendous sneezes herself—a Royal sized sneeze, Fanny called them to herself), she thought how much more Mrs Schellenbarter would disprove of her if she knew of Fanny's night-time excursions to the theatre.

The Royal family's terrace promenade was a popular sight, watched by townspeople and visitors alike. They stood on the grass and paving stones below where they could look up at the terraces on which King George and his family walked up and down. The Queen held the hand of the youngest princess, Amelia, while the others followed in twos: Princess Charlotte, the Princess Royal, Augusta, Elizabeth, Mary and Sophie.

The Prince of Wales, and the Dukes of Kent, Gloucester, Clarence and Cumberland, had left the Royal household as soon as they could and were rarely seen. Although Fanny believed that the Prince of Wales was expected on a visit soon. Everyone knew, from the Lord Chamberlain himself to the draymen of London, that he disliked his father and his father felt the same about him.

"Mr Pitt does not approve of this promenading," whispered Mr Smelt, gentleman in waiting. "Thinks it's dangerous, asking for trouble. A shot could be fired. Or a man could leap up on to the terrace and stab the King, but the King won't listen. Says he must show himself to his people... Only in good weather, though. I wish His Majesty felt the same about hunting, soaked through we were yesterday and obliged to say we enjoyed it. Upon my soul, it's a hard life we have here."

It was always hard to tell when Mr Smelt was joking or not.

"Mr Pitt, Mr Pitt," said Mrs Schellenbarter, with scorn. "Who is he?"

"The Prime Minister, that's who he is. William Pitt."

"William, what a name."

"We have had three Kings of that name, and might well have another," said Mr Smelt, who liked to bait Mrs S. This was what he called her among friends, but never to her face, she was too powerful a lady for that.

The band, of the Grenadier Guards whose tour of duty it was, having done full justice to God Save the King now struck into something strong by Handel.

The crowd below stared up to where the King, in his red coat and white britches, the Star of the Garter on his breast, made a perfect target for any marksman. Fanny could un-

16

derstand what worried Mr Pitt. Fanny said as much to Mr Smelt.

"But no Englishman would want to kill the King, that madwoman with the knife, yes, but no one else." Did she believe this? She was not sure.

"There are the French and the Americans."

"Oh since they are independent, the Americans have their own King now, they have George Washington."

"President, Fanny, president."

Fanny, standing motionless behind the Queen, assuaged her boredom by studying the faces of the crowd. She had another motive too, which she did not wish to think about.

More women than men, but this was usual. All well dressed, none really poor but not rich either. Shawls, bonnets and sturdy overshoes were the order of the day. Here and there a child was held up to get a good view of the Royal family. Some men, but not many.

She studied the men's faces. The man was there. Yes, there he was, here again, At the back of the ground but not hiding. He never hid; he wanted to be seen.

He stood there, a tall, badly dressed man yet not giving the impression of being a beggar, his shoulders were hunched, his back humped. Yes, he had a hump that his cloak masked but did not altogether hide. He had a hat pulled down over his face so one could never tell where his eyes were looking, but more and more with each time she saw him, Fanny had the uneasy impression that he was looking at her.

She turned her face away.

The band went back to playing a march as King George took his wife by her hand and led her, followed by the rest of his troupe, back into the castle.

It was an oddly theatrical performance as Fanny appreciated, and if the King had turned to the Queen as they went in and said: "A good house today, my dear," she felt

17

she would not have been surprised.

Since Fanny was the last, except for three footmen, to leave the terrace she was able to look back without Mrs S observing her.

The crowd had thinned, but the man was still there. And no doubt about it, he was now looking straight at Fanny. As a writer whose book had brought her fame, Fanny knew what it was to have strangers stare at her, even to come up to speak; but this man seemed different.

She caught his eye, for a moment they looked at each other directly.

—*Never look trouble in the eye*, her old nurse had said, *or trouble will look at you.*

Fanny felt a shiver run through her. She walked through the open doors into the Castle to see Mrs S frowning at her. Mr Smelt was studying her face also.

You never go unwatched in a Court.

"The Queen has offered me a place in one of the coaches to go to the Egham races," she said to Charlotte Minden that night, as she put on her cloak, drew the hood about her and prepared to go into the town.

"And will you go?"

"Yes. I think so. But I am not sure if I will be allowed by Mrs S."

Charlotte Minden, tall and handsome in her thick alpaca skirt and shawl (she wore no hoop, being a working woman) ignored this and said; "I was looking out of an upstairs window when the Terrace walk was on and I saw that man again."

"I saw him too. He was looking at me, I think." Fanny said this with no vanity.

"I think so too, miss."

"I try not to meet his eye," said Fanny slowly. "I would not know his face, and I am sure I do not wish to, but I know by the way he stands."

—We will have trouble for you, Miss Fanny Burney, thought Charlotte Minden, I feel it coming on.

For all that Miss Burney could be so quiet she did not lack admirers. Lord Frederic Bertie confessed to admiring her, he was a tall, elegant man, who was usually said to have a broken heart from some early romance, as he had never married. Certain, he took care to be in Miss Burney's company, although she was discreet in meeting his favours.

She likes him, I think, Charlotte Minden thought.

They left the castle by a quiet, dark side route. There was a soldier on duty at the picket gate, but he let them through with a nod to Charlotte but no sign of recognition to Fanny.

He knew her though, and would report back later that the two women had left the castle.

He leaned forward to the maid, whom he knew, as he closed the gate behind them, whispering a few words.

"What did he say?"

Charlotte walked on a few paces without answering.

"Come on, Charlotte... Mindy, tell me."

Then she said: "He told me that a woman had been killed in the town, left with her throat ripped open, and that we should take care."

"Did you believe him?"

"Soldier boys do have their jokes, but Tommy's not one for joking... Yes, I think I believed him."

"Where was this?"

"Peascod Street."

"Do they know who did it?"

"No, she was found in a door way."

Charlotte Minden stood there. "Do you want to go back, Miss?"

"No, I want to go to the theatre." Fanny's voice was determined. "This is work, not pleasure."

19

"Yes, miss." So you say, my dear miss.

"I mean to write a play, I *am* going to write a play, and I can't do that without watching other plays."

"He writes a good play, Mr Manston, I admit it, and he acts in it well too. Yes, he might make a good master."

"Oh Mindy, I could be angry with you. Mr Manston is nothing to me."

"Tell me what you fear most, Miss, to be raped or murdered?"

"Charlotte Minden!"

"This poor woman got both." Charlotte Minden gathered her cloak around her: "Forward it is then, miss, if you will and if I say run, then run."

There was something in her servant's voice that halted Fanny. "Mindy, you sound as if you know."

"What, miss?"

"Not about the killing, I don't mean that..." Fanny sought for words. "As if you knew what was it was like, had seen..." she stumbled into silence, seeing her maid's grim smile.

"I have never had my throat cut, miss."

"But you know." Fanny found the words to say.

"I have been raped, miss, yes. When I was eleven years old. My father sent me to work when I was eleven... don't blame him, miss, he had six more of us to feed and I was the eldest. He is a good father and he found me a good master and mistress... it was not their fault, life is rough in the docks."

They had stopped walking in the narrow lane that led to the old High Street, it was a cloudy night with a half moon.

"Do you want to know what it was like, miss?"

"Don't be angry, Mindy; I am so sorry."

"I am not angry but you only half know what life is really like."

"The castle," began Fanny. "It circumscribes one..."

"The castle, the castle," said Charlotte Minden with some force. "Do you think the castle is safe? What about the young princesses, with the footmen in and out of their rooms all the day? And no one there thinking of finding husbands for them. There is more than one way of getting a royal bastard."

"I never know when to take you seriously or not, Charlotte Minden."

"Take me seriously then. Being good and virtuous is not always a choosing for a woman, she can have her virtue snatched from her."

They walked on in silence.

Charlotte Minden shows me the dark side of life, Fanny was thinking. She is the dark side, but so full of courage. She is younger than I am, but has seen more of life, *real* life, than I have. She is braver too.

I think I could be brave, I must face things, not hide which is what I do now. About the princesses... surely not, And yet she may be right. I don't like many of the footmen myself. Suddenly, ahead of them, they saw the lamps of the theatre. A crowd was surging in to take their places. They bought their tickets from the man at the table at the door, and received their playbill with particulars of the whole evening's entertainment. You took your seat as you could find it. There was no reserving places in this theatre which was simple and unpretentious, although you could send a servant to keep your place. The Court was a strong patron. If the King wanted to see a play in Windsor, he called the company of players into the castle, or went himself to an ordinary public performance. The bill was changed daily.

The Royal Theatre was narrow and boxlike. The floor sloped towards the stage, lit by the rows of oil lamps which David Garrick had introduced to replace the candles floating in water in glass jars that were such a fire risk. Not that the oil lamps were without their dangers. If you smelt scorching wood and singeing baize, run, was what every theatregoer knew to do. Run or it might be too late.

Charlotte Minden, who was skilful in such matters, eased them into good seats in the circle. They sat on benches with a hard back, squeezed in between a fat woman with her spouse and a large thin man on the other side.

"If you'd let me come down early I could have got us good seats. Or you could have asked Peter to come." Peter was Fanny's footman.

"He is a gossip. And I wanted you with me. I don't like to walk through the town alone."

The maid was silent since these agreed with her own feelings. Someone like Fanny ought to be out with her own footman. She wondered sometimes what Fanny was really doing on these trips, sometimes twice a week if she could escape from the castle. Learning how to write a play? Or did she have some other interest? Charlotte Minden herself certainly had an interest beside Fanny: she liked the young stage-manager. A Londoner like herself who was learning his trade.

But I don't understand such things as writing and learning... I can write my name and that is it, but I understand things... down here. She touched her body below her waist. "I feel things." Sometimes a voice seemed to speak to her and she felt it came from somewhere in her gut.

And what she heard at the moment made her uneasy.

Fanny was reading the playsheet in the light of the great chandelier above her. First a farce, then a song and dance from the leading lady—it was to be hoped she could sing—and then the main play *The Rover* by Mrs Behn.

In the yellow light from above, Fanny's face looked tired and drawn.

Charlotte Minden had picked up a murmur that was going round the audience. A kind of sibilant hiss was passing from couple to couple. She leaned across to Fanny and whispered in her ear.

"It's the name of the murdered woman... she's an actress in this theatre."

Fanny stared, horror struck.

"Susan Sandys... we have seen her perform.

Back in the castle, in spite of their caution, their departure had been noted and it was known where they had gone.

This, and other matters, was being discussed in a quiet room in the Constable's tower.

In spite of some opposition from the King, Mr Pitt as Prime Minister, had insisted on setting up an investigating unit in the castle to protect the King and the security of the realm, a unit rather on the lines of the 'bureau d'investigation' soon to be created by Napoleon Bonaparte in Paris. One can learn from one's enemies. This unit was known simply as the Lower Room and in charge was Major Mearns, lately of his Majesty's army. He was assisted by Sergeant Denny. They had used the example of the police force set up in London by Sir John Fielding, using informers while working with the local magistrates and JP.

They had heard of the murder of the young actress Susan Sandys; knew of it before Fanny Burney and Charlotte heard. Knew more of it, too.

"And we know she was not the first," said the Major, "we have had one here in the Castle."

"Nor likely to be the last."

"No."

And raped too. Not with a male member but with an instrument. Bad, both men thought.

Although both of the army, they had experience of crime

23

and murder in the Great Wen, the city of London.

"Once a killer like that starts, he carries on, gets a taste for it. We have seen it before. I remember in Madras…"

"Yes, sir, and it was a colour sergeant of ours."

'Ours', the regiment they shared, was the Royal Madras Horse.

They were both strongly built, muscular men, but not heavy since horses, even horses bred for battle, perform better when not weighed down too much.

"All the same," said the sergeant, "no danger to the King in it."

"You take too limited a view, Denny. A run of murders, women killed in an unsavoury way, and there might be disorders in Windsor."

"Not a riot, sir."

"Possible, possible, and then there might be a threat to the King, and to the Queen… Look at France."

There was no denying that events in France, the fall of Louis XVII and his wife Queen Marie Antoinette and the arrival of a revolutionary government had made the Court and the Tory government profoundly uneasy. Disorder, revolution, like a terrible infection, could spread by contagion.

"Denny, in a better world you would be the Major and I would be the Sergeant."

"Yes sir." Sergeant Denny was decisive.

This is the note of their relationship, brisk, matter of fact, equal as men but accepting rank and status with a sceptical smile.

"But as it is, I am and you are not."

The performance was about to begin. A party of people had managed to find seats upon the stage itself, a practice that the actor manager David Garrick had forbidden at Drury Lane ever since Mrs Siddons had to fight her way through a great crowd in order to play Juliet. The provincial theatres still allowed it on occasion and Mr Hill, the proprietor of the Windsor theatre let his friends sit there if he was in a good mood or if he owed a tradesman a favour, he was very often a late payer of his bills.

The farce began. Fanny studied the play sheet: Mr Manston as the bridegroom, Miss Headington as the bride.

A two hander, then. A ripple of applause as Mr Manston appeared, through the side door near the boxes, he was handsome with a deep, rich voice. He bowed, then turned as Miss Headington came tripping in. She too was popular, getting her round, with even a cheer or two from the back benches where the apprentice boys and the soldier lads and the grooms from the castle bestowed themselves.

"My love," began Mr Manston, fixing his eyes, oddly, not on the fair face of Miss Headington, but Fanny, who blushed.

Charlotte admired Fanny for the blush, it was a feat to blush when you had come here to see Mr Manston and be stared at from the stage. Miss Headington had also stared at an admirer, but she had not blushed.

They were acting a love affair but not looking at each other. That must be why it is called a farce, thought Charlotte.

The farce ended and Mr Hill appeared on the stage through the door.

In a sombre voice as he removed his hat, he told the audience that they would have heard of the sad death of Miss Susan Sandys, their admired comic actress, that he had not cancelled tonight's performance because he knew Miss Sandys would not wish them to be disappointed.

—Nor lose his pennies for the night, thought Charlotte Minden cynically. She knew a bit about Mr Hill.

But tomorrow, announced Mr Hill, there would be a benefit for Miss Sandys' daughter and husband. Tickets would be available from Mrs Sandys' lodgings in South Street. Mr Hill bowed, and left the stage.

The next performance was a charming song and dance, if a little dirgelike by Miss Headington. She made a musical request that "In sad cypress let me be laid." Everyone knew it was in memory of Miss Sandys.

There was a short pause during which Fanny murmured to Charlotte that she must seek some fresh air. Together they pushed their way through the orange sellers with the trays suspended from the waist and the hot chestnuts man with his bucket of hot coals and the pokes of frozen coloured water called hokey-pokey. The ice seller pushed a small white cart with a huge block of ice on it on a metal tray with the frozen water imbedded in it in a jug. The ice came from the icehouse in the castle, provided by one of the butlers for cash to a fish seller in the town and then bits sold on to the iceman. The pokes were popular with the soldiers and the lads in the gallery.

As they made their way back into the theatre to see the main play: *The Rover* by Mrs Behn, a theatre usher came up to Fanny, bowed, and said:

"Mr Manston would be glad if you would take refreshment with him in his dressing-room after the play."

Fanny smiled and nodded. "Tell him, we shall be delighted," she looked at Mindy under her lashes, with the subtle, steely determined look that the servant knew. Not many saw that look but Mindy saw it often.

"Should we go? Suppose the Queen should ask for you."

"She won't, she gave me my freedom this evening."

But not to go out on the town, thought Mindy. "The streets will be dark."

"Mr Manston will send a servant home with us." Or come himself, as Fanny dared to hope.

The play, although eagerly anticipated by Fanny, if not her maid, seemed to drag.

GWENDOLINE BUTLER

The leading comic part was played by Mr Hill himself.
He walked and promenaded himself with gusto. When he
forgot his lines he looked at the ceiling, then at the audience, and gave them a joke. They usually laughed with
him, they knew his jokes.

Half way through, after he had stamped around the stage
more heavily than usual, the great chandelier, above the
stage, fell slowly down and settled on his shoulders so that
he was ringed in candles. He appeared as if some classical
sacrifice, mouth open, eyes popping.

He got a good laugh at that. Two stage helpers rushed
forward to put the candles out while lifting off his wig. Mr
Hill staggered off, returning soon, dampened down but
still smoking slightly.

The play went on.

At the end, Fanny shrugged.

"I never was more bored in my life, except when the
chandelier fell down, now that was good. Did you see his
face? I think his wig was singeing as they rushed forward
to put him out," said the forthright Mindy as she walked
behind her. "But otherwise, I was bored. No, I tell a lie: I
was more bored at the Dean's sermon last Sunday."

They were greeted warmly by Mr Manston whose dressing room was cosy with candlelight.

"Miss Burney, a pleasure." He handed her a glass of wine.
"My man will be along with some coffee from the coffee
house in Ship Street." He shook his head. "We were flat
tonight, very flat." He held up the wine, studying the colour in the light of the nearest candle. "It was a poor house."

A tall, fair-haired man, standing in the corner, shook his
head. "We should have closed, the house should have been
dark. Everyone felt the loss of Susan."

Mr Manston held out his hand towards the man. "Winter Ames, our American."

Winter Ames bowed towards Fanny. "And you are the

27

famous Miss Burney: I am honoured."

"Winter is an unusual name."

"Winterton, in truth, but this is overlong for a playbill."
He was a tall, slender man with bright blue eyes, and fair
hair with a touch of red.

"Winter is my American cousin, over with me to do some
acting and write a play perhaps. One of the first American
plays, Winter?"

"There will soon be others. Acted over here, perhaps."

"We won't ask King George to see it."

"The play went badly," said Fanny. "I expected better of
Mrs Behn."

Winter said in his slow, deep voice. "That may be due to
the fact that Mr Hill prides himself on never learning his
lines, never even looking at them but making them up as
he goes along, and never attending a rehearsal himself."

Fanny laughed, her eyes met Winter's, then looked towards Mr Manston's more sombre gaze. A shiver ran
through her and not from fear.

"I believe I am a very passionate person," she told herself.

Through a confusion of feelings, she heard the door open
and the noise of china and the smell of coffee.

"Ah, Bates, here you are with the coffee. Miss Burney,
will you take some?"

Bates advanced, then his hand shook so that coffee
spilled. He took a step back.

"Bates... indeed, watch what you do."

"Oh miss, forgive me... just for a moment... it was a
shock... You have such a look of Miss Sandys... you could
be sisters."

In their private hideaway, the Major turned to Sergeant
Denny.

"Take your boots off the firedog and get out to see if the

two girls are back. I want to know. What a pair. There's more goes on there than the dear Queen knows."

The Sergeant put on his boots, flaming hot they were. "Right, I'll be off."

He strode away. He was interested in the two young women, more personally interested in Charlotte Minden, perhaps.

TWO

Fanny and Charlotte Minden were seen back to the castle by the two men, James Manston and Winter Ames who walked on either side of them up the castle hill.

"Stupid fellow, Bates," said Manston. "Saying what he did. I should dismiss him." He had no intention of doing so; Bates was far too useful. And, although he never admitted this even to himself, knew far too much about Manston's life and feelings about women.

"Not on my account," Fanny said at once. "He meant no harm to me."

Blood could run, thought Mindy, before that young lady would admit to seeing it.

They passed Lord Frederic Bertie riding his black into the town. He looked surprised to see Fanny in the company she was, but bowed and smiled. He was always elegant, a tall, handsome young man.

"Oh there's Freddie Bertie," said James Manston. "Always a pleasure. Handsome isn't he?" He seemed likely to pause, and meditate on this beauty.

Fanny flushed: she knew, or thought she knew, that Lord Frederic admired her. But he was one of those young men who appear and disappear, seemingly into other lives.

Charlotte Minden look over. "I will see Miss Burney the last few yards... there is the guard at the door, we

31

are safe enough." And it was better not to let him see the two young women walk up with their escorts. Mindy knew this soldier, he was a decent man, but everything got reported and gossiped about at court.

She thought she saw the shadow of the man she knew as the Sergeant disappearing round a corner now. The castle was so full of dark corners; anyone could hide, and listen.

She had observed the Major and the Sergeant walking about the castle, almost as if it was their castle and not the King's, and wondered about them, they seemed a pair. Rather like a pair of old gloves, of which you had lost one, matched it with another to make a working set. She had watched to see where they went. She had never achieved this; they had a knack of disappearing at the end of a corridor into distant space.

There he went now. But at least she was beginning to have some idea where he was going. That corridor ended in a staircase, winding and dim, up which she had never gone, but the sergeant had. So not into space.

No, into some useful set of rooms and anterooms in which the castle abounded. That was the answer.

But what was their purpose? She was sure they had one, and watching people came into it. Her early experience around the docks of London had introduced her to men like this before. Sometimes they were the leader of press gangs, looking for men to force into the navy. Sometimes they were men of the new police invented by the blind Magistrate Fielding to protect the law courts of London—although such did not often venture into the land of wharves and docks which had their own guards.

The castle, however, with all the soldiers and courtiers, did not need policemen, surely?

Mindy walked behind Fanny as was good manners

once inside the castle when she went back to being just Miss Fanny's maid. Outside, she felt her equal, indeed, in sharpness and strength, her superior, but Fanny was a lady, although a remarkably clever one, which made a difference. Not always open, kept things to herself, but easily read as to motives and emotions by her loyal servant Mindy. Three years in her service and never a blow or a cross word. Mindy knew she had a good place, but she knew her own worth too. She knew her own temper as well, and a rough word or a slap might have got the same back and then what was there for a servant girl, but dismissal in disgrace and the streets.

As she undressed her mistress for the night, she said: "Two fine young men, miss."

Fanny nodded absently.

"But don't trust the older one, Mr Manston. He has a cold and sweaty hand when he puts it on your shoulder. Never trust a man with a cold and sweaty hand, miss." This was not true of the Major or Sergeant Denny.

"No?" said Fanny, still absently. "I suppose you know, Mindy."

"Aye, I do." Also he is older than he looks.

On all these points, Mindy knew she was a sure guide. Sergeant Denny disappeared into the quiet room where he found the Major reading a newspaper brought from London by the King's messenger and drinking a pint of porter.

"Home and dry," he said.

"Where did they go?"

"The theatre. As per usual..." He dragged out the last syllable. "She's sweet on Manston, I perspect."

"Suspect, use English, Denny."

"Suspect, perspect, as the words come to mind, but what I say is so. And there's trouble for her there if she takes it serious."

"So you think."

"So I know, sir. Manston has a woman in every town, and the odd young lad too, for he is not partial as to sex. And what he does with them is worth a question."

"Is that so."

"You know so, sir, for did you not warn him off your young nephew."

Major Mearns put his newspaper down. "You were not supposed to know of that."

"No keeping secrets from me, sir."

"I had noticed."

"I don't like Manston. A fidgety fellow."

The Major did not enquire what the sergeant meant by this, thinking that it might suit him if Manston was fidgeted indeed, but said:

"I think Miss Burney could be useful to us, close to the Queen, a young woman with eyes and ears. Have you read her book?"

Denny shook his head. He liked to read the London *Times* when the Major had done with it, and enjoyed *The Berkshire Gazette* and the more gossipy and scandalous *Langley Looseleaf*, but he was not a great book man.

"She sees into the dark side of life, her imagination plumbs the depths."

"I think the maid is the sharper of the two."

"Yes, that may well be, and we can tap into her, but the other has the imagination."

"She's watched, you know," said Sergeant Denny suddenly. "A man comes to the castle grounds when the King goes walking and onlookers are allowed. He watches her, not the King. I think she has begun to notice."

Major Mearns was silent for a few minutes. "Did you pick up anything about the death of Miss Sandys?"

Denny pursed his lips. "Nothing except some talk of

34

her looking like Miss Burney…"

"Which is true enough."

The two men exchanged a thoughtful look.

"And the other death, the girl Sophy Todd, no one talks much of her because she was a lady of the town. But she was stabbed, and she too was fair and pale, and not unlike Miss Sandys, who was not unlike Miss Burney."

The Major began to walk around the room, wagging his right forefinger as he went. "Miss Burney, eh?"

"So do we have a killer who wants to kill young wimmin who look so?"

"Could be, could be."

"Or just getting practice before Miss Burney?"

Major Mearns took a turn around the room in silence. "We may not know until too late, Denny," he said, at last.

"I'll work on Mindy Minden," said the sergeant. "Tens to one, she knows more than she says."

"I think Miss Burney may also, that imagination of hers will be telling her."

"But she does not know about Sophy Todd."

"Who's to say, she doesn't?" If Mindy Minden knew, then the chances were she had told her mistress. "I mean to find out more about Sophy Todd and also Susan Sandys… a married woman, I believe, with a child. Husbands can be killers. I shall see the Magistrate to-morrow. Give him a drink in the Castle, he will not take that amiss."

Fanny and Mindy let themselves into Fanny's apartment.

"A dish of tay, miss?"

Fanny opened her mouth to say No, thank you, but she saw that Mindy was in earnest. Perhaps she needed a drink herself, or more likely, seeing her intent gaze, she wanted to talk.

"Thank you, yes. Take it with me."

Mindy bobbed. "Thank you, miss. Shall I help you into your robe?"

"No, Mindy, I can do it myself. But I am tired, I admit. Apart from everything I went down to take Mary Diggens some clothing for the child."

"You've been down to that Bell Yard," said Mindy with some anger.

"Lower Bell Yard."

"Lower Bell Yard or Upper Bell Yard, it's not for you, Miss."

Fanny had been trying to bring some comfort into the deprived life of Mary Diggens, a widow, penniless, who was living in a crowded tenement with her four children. The baby was sickening with something. A fever of some sort.

"Well, all the more reason to keep away," said the unsympathetic Mindy.

Fanny did not answer. Lower Bell Yard puzzled and worried her, she was not unused to such work, but Mrs Diggens' crowded room had now a lodger. On this occasion, she had seen a man rolled in an old blanket sleeping on the floor.

Mrs Diggens said he was her brother Nick. He did any work he could find, but at the moment, he had none. If Miss Burney could...

"I will do what I can," Fanny had said. "Rough work, I suppose?"

The man stirred himself and looked at her, straight, unsmiling. "Rough enough, miss," he had said. "Sometimes the rougher the better. I sell my services for what I can get, ma'am."

Mindy interrupted her thoughts.

"I will just puff up the fire and put the kettle on." Making tea in the Castle, in any castle, was not easy at night: the fire must be persuaded to burn up, the kettle must be put on the trivet over the fire, and brought to the boil.

Fanny had brought some delicate Worcester cups and saucers with her from London, while the teapot was round and silver like a small cannon ball.

"I must get some more water."

"Do that, Mindy." There was no water on this floor; Mindy must go down to the kitchens.

She sat by the fire, listening to its pleasant crackle; Mindy had disappeared and would be gone some time, the kitchens were not close. Fanny's thoughts were sombre. Although she had brushed aside the man Bates' cry that how like to the murdered woman she was, she knew it was so.

She picked up the little hand looking glass to see how she looked for Mindy had undone the pins in her hair to let it run free on her shoulders. "I knew it before," she said to her face. "I thought it when I saw you act, but it did not seem important then. In fact, you are" — she corrected herself— "you were prettier than me." Perhaps not so pretty now.

Mindy came hurrying back and soon had the tea made which she poured carefully, then handed the delicate cup to Fanny. "East west, tea is best."

"Where did you hear that?"

"Made it up. No, tell a lie, it goes round the kitchens down below." She leaned forward to pour her own tea, then replace the teakettle on the fire. "There are kitchens and kitchens down there, and pantry upon pantry. And three rooms just for making tea." She laughed.

"It is a royal palace," said Fanny wearily.

"Oh nothing is in the common way of things here, I

know that, miss. It's a town, a city in itself, a world."

"Yes, so it is." Fanny sipped her tea.

"Two worlds, the one on top where the royals live and such as you, Miss Fanny, and the underneath world where there's drinking and fighting and wenching."

"Mindy, mind your tongue."

"You know it, miss, as well as I do, but you never say. And so to murder, miss, for there's been one in the town, of which you know, and one in the castle."

Mindy sat back, watching Fanny's face, she was satisfied, "Pricked her at last, thank God."

"Here? I can hardly believe it. I would have heard. So would the Queen."

"Don't you believe that, miss. There's plenty goes on the Queen never gets to hear. But there's a reason the death wasn't talked about."

"But you know." Fanny put a slight but definite emphasis on you.

"That's different... people like me get to know things." The gossip in the lower regions of the castle was swift and constant: all stories were known and passed round. Added to, as a rule, as the conveyer of the tale thought fit or was able to invent. The Royal family would have been shocked if they had known how well documented and assessed they were downstairs. Probably the Prince of Wales and his elder brothers had some idea of how they were talked about, and accurately too. Although the King and Queen may have got the whiff of it at times, they did not know the sharp accuracy of the observations which were handed on.

All the same, things got hidden, lost in the castle... a body could lie there, rotting, for weeks before anyone discovered it.

Had done.

"Why, Mindy," her friend, the old pantryman called

Groovey, had said, "There he was, this poor dead sod. We did wonder who was polishing the silver, which he should have been doing, but we just moved on, plenty of silver on the shelves in the silver pantry, and he'd hanged himself in the basement middy. There's always a stink from there, so we thought nothing of it and just took our comfort elsewhere."

Hanged dead, and left to rot. Any number also of rats, cats, and even the odd dog. You looked where you walked, Mindy wanted to say, in the basements of the castle.

Should she say anything to Fanny? In time, thought Mindy, but not yet.

"You speak as if we do not live in the same world."

Do we? "It's a full moon tonight, miss. Have you ever walked round the town in the full moon?"

Fanny stared. "Yes, of course, the moon helps you to see."

"And what did you see, miss? Did you go round the alleys off Fleet Street and Bridesgate and see the people coupling against the walls, and the dead baby in the sewer that runs down the middle of the street, and think to yourself is that baby dead or just drowning, because the two against the wall with their humping and heaving don't care?"

"Mindy!"

"Ay, Mindy! You don't know the world you live in, miss."

"More than you think. One reads and learns. The wind blows on us all, Mindy."

"Reads and learns," said Mindy with force. "There are smells and sounds the wind never brought to you, miss, but I have smelt them, all but tasted them."

She could see that Fanny's face was white, but she felt only a little remorse: Fanny must see, must understand the world she lived in. So clever with her writing, so blind to what was around her.

Mindy picked up the pot, touched it to see if it was still hot. "More tea, miss?" She took the cup from Fanny's unresisting hand and poured out the tea, then handed the cup back to Fanny.

Fanny sipped; the colour came back into her face. "I know more than I talk about, Mindy. I am not as ignorant as you think. I do not need my eyes open quite so much." She shook her head while she managed a smile. "I thought I was educating you, Mindy, bringing you here, but I can see you mean to be the teacher." She put the cup down. "You know, I think this is how revolutions start: with people like you busy telling the truth about the world as they see it."

"That's being clever, Miss Fanny, now be clever about yourself. I think you are in danger: one woman has been killed who looks like you, there was another, the first as far as I know, killed here in the castle."

"Did she look like me?"

"Yes. When alive. She worked in the kitchens, on and off, lived in the town... but died here."

"I am not sure if I understand you, Mindy... Was she killed instead of me or because women with my looks are licensed to be killed?"

"That is clever talk, miss... That is how Sergeant Denny works it out."

"And who is Sergeant Denny?"

"He and the Major... Major Mearns... they are watchers, they watch for danger. They think I don't know them but I have rousted out their names and who they are."

"And they think I am in danger?"

"You may be, Miss Fanny."

Fanny stared at the teacup. "I had better go to bed

then, so I can be ready for whatever comes. I am still the Queen's dresser, remember, and she will not like it if I am fretful and tired."

"You don't believe me, miss, do you?"

"No, I think you have been reading too many of those new tales of horror."

"And what about the dead woman, murdered woman?"

Fanny yawned. "I shall get you to write a play, Mindy, you have the imagination for it, perhaps more than I have... the dead women are nothing to do with me."

She moved across the room into the dark away from the fire and candles. Fanny walked slowly towards the table by the window in the darkest spot of all. Mr Manston had thrust a note into her hand as they parted which she had held in her hand and put on the table when she came into the room. Not a piece of behaviour that she would have praised in the heroine in her novel but she wanted now to read the note.

A protestation of love? A plea for a meeting?

She put her hand out to pick up the note, in the dark could hardly see but she soon felt that she had put her hand on to something wet.

"Mindy, it's wet here, has something been spilt?"

"Not that I know of, miss."

Fanny touched her right hand with her left hand... now both felt wet to the touch. Sticky wet.

"Bring a candle."

"I am doing." Mindy hurried towards her with the candle from the mantelshelf. She held the light so that it shone on Fanny's hands. "Here, let's have a look. What is it you've got on your hands?"

"I touched the table."

Mindy raised the candle so the light shone on the table. "There is blood, a pool of blood."

Fanny stared from the table to her hands, "How could that be?"

"There's plenty of places to get blood. The butcher for one, and from a stabbed person if you happen to have a basin close at hand to catch what falls." Mindy's voice was grim, but she was shining the candle further along the table. "Here's a rag soaked in red... but I think water is there too... blood and water, which is why it is so liquid, for blood does not stay like that but thickens as it dries."

Fanny said, in distress: "But how did it get there?"

"It was put there."

"But here? And how? This is the castle, and where the King lives. How could anyone do it?" Fanny was almost in tears; her hands were shaking.

"By someone who walked in, miss. Anyone can get into the castle if they try and, when in, walk about freely. It's like a city, miss." Mindy sounded abstracted. "I wonder if we should get the sergeant? From what I see of him, I believe he is the man to go for."

Fanny stood there holding out her blood stained hands, while Mindy still stared at the table.

"Whoever he is, he left a knife behind," she said, holding the candle high above her head so that the light flickered on the metal blade and the dark shaft.

Whoever he was, he knew what he was doing.

He who had left the blood and the knife, in that order, because the blood seemed more important as a symbol and a warning, was still in the castle grounds, He had watched Fanny and Mindy come back together.

There was no thought in his mind of molesting either young woman. That would come later.

The serving girl was an enticing item, but her looks were against her. She could be left aside for the moment, but the other one... ah, she was the one. Made for what he had in mind.

They do not know what I am, he told himself, where he rested in the shadows of the castle wall. I am a man of these times, I am an icon.

This is a time of revolution and I am a revolutionary. It is my revolution.

He said the words aloud. The moon came out from behind the clouds so that the shadow capering behind him was like a dog, and his laughter like a bark.

Sergeant Denny, looking out of his window on to the courtyard, before turning in for his nights rest, saw nothing. Not even a shadow moving.

THREE

Fanny was up early in spite of her late night. She dressed rapidly, because with Mrs S ill (if she was indeed ill—Fanny thought her a malingerer), it fell to Fanny to assist in the Queen's dressing before the early morning service in the Chapel Royal, which the Queen always attended. Fanny found herself wishing the Queen was less devout. It was duty she thought, rather than devotion. There was an innocence about Queen Charlotte however that precluded too much criticism.

Fanny buried all this inside herself while she dragged on her clothes, helped by Mindy. "No, I will not wear a hoop so early in the day, if the Queen thinks she must do to go to Chapel, that is for her, but I will not."

Accordingly, she scuttled through the windy corridors to the royal apartments with her skirts flapping about her.

Mindy shrugged, nothing would make Miss Burney attend to fashion. Still shrugging, she made her way to the sinks and the washplace so that she could rinse out the towels with which she had mopped out the blood of yesterday night.

Wash it out, but not to forget it. What did Fanny think of it in the light of morning? They had not talked about it, but it was surely not forgotten. Mindy could see it

45

was not, in the paleness of Fanny's face and the sober set to her lips.

Mindy stood at the sink with her back to the door so that although she heard footsteps she did not know who had come in. One of the cleaning maids who might be reprimanded for the poor state of the sink. She turned round.

Sergeant Denny stood at the door, a towel draped across his arm, he was obviously about to wash and shave at one of the row of basins that stretched across one wall. He looked at the bloody water in Mindy's basin but said nothing.

Mindy turned back to her washing, also without speaking. She could see that although she had rinsed out the blood, that the stain remained. This did not matter, the towel could be thrown away. Boiling it would be no good, the stain would set firmly, but what did matter was where did the blood come from? How was a question easily enough answered as she reminded herself: someone walked into the castle and walked through the corridors to find Fanny Burney's room.

Why? Not for love, Mindy thought.

She looked up and once again met the Sergeant's eyes. "Blood." he said.

"So it is." said Mindy.

"I know you: you are Charlotte Minden and you serve Miss Fanny Burney."

Mindy considered. "I believe I have heard you called Sergeant Denny."

"That I am. Late of His Majesty's army."

A well set up man, Mindy decided, not so young, but not old either. Soldiers are aged by their life. He had fought, been wounded perhaps, and survived. A survivor herself, she found that attractive.

"The blood," she began, wondering if she should go on.

"Seen plenty of it in my time."

So have I, though Mindy, in the streets of Clerkenwell.

"The blood was found, a pool of it, in Miss Burney's room, on the table she uses to dress her hair." Mindy added: "I think it was blood and water. So it would not go thick."

"Blood will thicken if left long."

"This was not left very long, say some four hours or less. It was not there when we went out to the theatre. But why was it there? And whose hand put it there."

"The cloth?" asked the sergeant.

"One of Miss's. I used it to mop up."

He stretched out his hand. "Give it to me."

"It's very stained, I can't think it will tell us any-thing... I was going to burn it."

"You may do that later, Miss Minden."

The towel went into his capacious hand. He exam-ined it. "Better if you had not washed it, perhaps."

"The linen belongs to Miss," Mindy protested.

"We might have learnt something. Objects can tell a story if you know how to look... when you mopped up the blood, who knows what you mopped up besides."

"No one's head or hands," said Mindy sharply.

"A fleck of this, or chip of this not easily seen except a magnifying glass and which might then suggest... sug-gest where the blood came from or who left it."

"I am sorry I washed it then."

"If I examined where the blood was...?"

"I should have to ask my mistress," said Mindy firmly.

Sergeant Denny accepted this, the more so since he could get in for a look whenever he chose.

"I would like you to meet my guv'nor, the Major."

Mindy considered: she wanted to meet the Major, but she was not going to rush into anything.

"I am busy all day... Helping Miss into her dress which

she must always be changing, washing her linen."

"In the evening?" queried the Sergeant, "still busy then?"

Mindy made up her mind: "Miss takes tea with Lady Hinde today, I am free then. Where does the Major lodge?" That would be interesting to know in itself, although no doubt one of the pantry boys or underfootmen who courted her favour would be able to tell her.

"In the nether regions," said the Sergeant, jovially, "he is like Beelzebub. I will wait for you here and take you." He bowed: "Miss Minden."

Mindy curtsied. "After all," she decided, as she rose, "I like being at court. It is making a lady of me—I must model myself on Lady Jersey, I think."

That lady had recently been at Windsor, and Mindy had seen her from a window as she arrived. She was thin, tall and elegant. 'A beautiful serpent,' someone had said in Mindy's hearing, 'and with the tongue of one.' —No bad thing to be at court, Mindy had thought.

Both Fanny and Mindy had their little arrangements to make that evening.

"The white sarsenet, please, Mindy," Fanny said. "Oh, this constant dressing in fiddle faddle... still you have it nicely done, Mindy, you must have been busy all day."

"So I have." The conversation with the sergeant, and the plans to meet the Major were her own affair.

"No more blood?" Fanny looked around the room. "A mystery, and not one I like, but who could I talk to? No one talks of blood in front of the Queen, of course, and Mrs S is ill, no friend to me anyway. There was Mr Smelt, but he is with the King, who is ill, wild and rambling. I could write to my father, but Dr Burney..." She shook her head.

Dr Burney would be no more help than a dead cat,

thought Mindy. A man of great kindness of heart and sweetness of manners but in the matter of death, except to arrange the funeral music, of no use at all. No, it's Sergeant Denny and the Major, I trust to.

"There is talk about the dead woman," said Fanny, studying her face in the looking glass. "Whispered talk that she was... well, a lady of no great virtue as well as being an actress."

Silently, Mindy handed her wig to Fanny. "Are you ready to powder?"

"Not just yet." Fanny got up and started to walk around the room. "Oh what a bore this powdering is. It's done with in France, you know, hair is loose and free. I daresay we shall follow suit..."

"Without a Revolution and a Dr Guillotine."

"Dr Seaton came to the Queen," said Fanny, coming at last to what she wanted to say. "He had some potion for her, she has a migraine... On the way out, he talked to me and Lady Shelter... she took Mrs Schellenbarter's duties... He said that the woman who was killed would not be the last." Fanny paused. "Nor had she been the first... he said these things went in a run where madness was concerned."

"Madness?"

"He used that word..." Fanny dropped her voice. "And as I walked to the door with him as is my duty to do, he whispered to me that it would be a terrible business if the King should have escaped and got into the town in his frenzy."

Mindy's eyes were round. "The King! But he couldn't, he couldn't leave the castle without being noticed."

"Oh he could, Mindy, he likes to be alone, sometimes he chases all his attendants away."

"But they stay outside his rooms."

"Not always, and think of the doors and ways out, so

many—it is like a warren. Remember the King was a boy here, he knows all the ways."

Mindy considered the case of the woman killed in the castle; left there, rotting, to be found when days had passed. Fair, young and pretty once. Who was she, that woman? A woman of the street who had wandered in. But perhaps she had been brought in.

Fanny took Mindy by the hand.

"That was not all... Dr Seaton reminded me how the King had always spoken to me with kindness and that it was his wish I should come to court."

Fanny covered her face with her hands. "I must not think it, of the King, I must shut out that picture."

A bell rang in the room next door. It always rang when Fanny was wanted, which was quite often. Fanny was never under any illusion that, although at Court, she was anything but a servant who must soon go to help an old lady put on her stockings.

Fanny started. "I am summoned." Hurriedly, they got Fanny into her clothes so that she could run, as she usually did, through the long corridors.

Over her shoulder as she fled, she said: "I am going to take tea with Lady Shelter, so you are free."

"Miss," called Mindy quickly, "that green cashmere shawl... may I borrow it?"

"It is yours," and Fanny was gone.

Mindy tidied the room, leaving it neat, and left in her turn with the shawl, over her arm. She intended to look fine for the Major.

She spent the day at her usual routine of laundering Miss Fanny's clothes, then pressing them with a hot iron. She was so deep in thought that she scorched a white muslin undershift, but Fanny would have to forgive her. If indeed she noticed; Fanny was more short sighted than she realised and saw less than there was to see, which Mindy had found useful in the past.

By the time that it was dusk, Mindy was ready to change her dress for the evening. She liked clothes, but had always been short of money, but the Burney household were generous at Christmas and Easter with presents of clothes.

She folded the green shawl about her shoulders, then set off down the corridors to where she expected to meet Sergeant Denny.

He was there before, stocky and bright eyed. "Here you are then, miss. And looking a picture if I may say so."

"You may," said Mindy. "And more than once if you like."

"There's no stopping you, is there?" He sounded cheerful. He offered his arm. "Let me take you to the Major."

Mindy looked about with interest. The castle was so large and complicated that she was finding whole corridors and staircases she had never seen before.

To be sure they were much of a muchness: the upper floors where the Royal family lived were carpeted with pictures on the walls which were lined with handsome cabinets and chairs. The lower floors were plainer, with unpolished wooden floors and even stone which was hard and cold to the feet. Down there you could forget being in a royal palace and remember that this was a castle which had known battle and even yet had soldiers stationed in it.

As well as odd couples like the Major and his Sergeant. Mindy had learnt enough of the world on the streets of London to sum up the pair as rum.

The room to which Sergeant Denny led her was long and narrow with a fire at one end. A door in the inner wall led to another room, the Major's sleeping room, she assumed. Two armchairs stood by the fire, close at hand a table with food and drink on it.

Two small windows on the wall opposite the door by which they had entered overlooked a quadrangle.

The Major saw her studying the room. "So miss, what do you make of us?"

Mindy took him in calmly. "Well sire, you are called Major, so you are a soldier, but you have a look of Bow Street Runner about you."

The Major laughed. "Well done, miss. Sharply observed. You have seen a Bow Street Runner then?"

Mindy bowed her head as if to say Yes. Indeed she had seen a Runner and more than one when she lived with her father. It had been what you might call "running country" there. "But there is something else," she went on, "you are a Major which means you are a gentleman but do not talk like Captain Lofts or Lieutenant Foster who I see with Miss Burney."

The Major clapped his hands. "Well done again, miss. Don't you think so, Denny?"

"She's as sharp as a needle, sir."

The Major swung back to Mindy. "Come and sit by the fire and let us talk."

Mindy stood where she was. "Some explanation first, Major sir."

"Where shall I begin, eh Denny?"

"Where it suits you, sir," said that man stolidly.

"I joined the army as a private, fought in America, came home, fought in Flanders. Became a sergeant, then was given the King's commission in the field for work behind the line."

"Behind the line and in front of it," said Denny, still stolidly.

"Right, right. I gathered information. So there you have it."

That's the Bow Street Runner side, thought Mindy, but there is something else as well. But I shall come to it, I will watch and listen and out what else there is about this man, whether good or bad I cannot yet tell.

Major Mearns was looking at Mindy as if he found her puzzling too. A treasure possibly, but a puzzling one too.

"Mr Pitt, our Prime Minister, has entrusted me with the task of protecting the King… looking around, you know, and observing the countryside as it were. You get used to doing that on a campaign in the army."

—That may be part of what I notice, thought Mindy, but not all. More to come.

"So why do you want to talk to me?"

"You are well placed in the castle to hear what goes on, Miss Burney so close to the Queen and so well liked by His Majesty and the young princesses. You can be my ear."

—Part of the truth thought Mindy, but not all of it. Never mind, I shall find out.

"My mistress does not gossip."

"No, nor do you, miss, I rely on your discretion. But you get to know things." And he put his finger to his nose and winked.

"For instance, you know the young actress who has been killed."

"By sight," said Mindy with caution.

"Slender, about the same height as your mistress, something like her?"

"Something," said Mindy with even more caution. "If you say so."

"I do say so. Would you be willing to look at the first young woman found dead?"

"The one found here, in the castle?"

The Major bowed.

"Is she still here?"

"We have a mortuary in the castle basement... and the Watcher is with her."

The Watcher was the respectable, elderly woman who received the corpse, washed it and did whatever was needed for decorum and seemliness.

"Why must I do this looking at her?"

"To see what you think she looks like."

Mindy made up her mind. "Will you pay me if I do it?"

Major Mearns shook his head. "No. There is no payment."

"Good." Mindy spoke with decision. "I should not come if it was a matter of payment."

"Some debts are better left unpaid." he answered gravely. Without more ado, he turned to the sergeant. "Lead the way Denny."

Sergeant Denny looked at Mindy. "A little brandy before we go, miss?"

Mindy refused. She set her teeth and marched forward, the Sergeant hurried after her and the Major came last. "The Sergeant will show the way."

Denny took Mindy's arm. "Just to direct you, miss," he said politely. "It's so mighty dark. Now, down this corridor, down this staircase. Watch your step."

They seemed to go down and down, with a smell of earth dampness rising up to them. It was indeed dark, with a light shining from a door at the bottom.

A short old lady stood at the door, she was waiting for them with a candle. She looked cheerful and alert, which surprised Mindy but as they got closer the whiff of gin hinted at the source of the jollity.

—Can't blame her, Mindy thought, it's desperate cold down here.

"Come at last," said the old lady to the Major.

"Right you are, Mrs Minchin."

"She's to be taken away today to be buried in Pauper's Plot so you are just in time."

"We are never late," said Sergeant Denny, bustling forward. Since he had himself arranged the burial date there was no surprise for him.

Mrs Minchin replied with a string of words all beginning with B or C. Mindy had been familiar from childhood with all swear words but she had never heard them delivered in so affectionate and gin-laden a manner.

The flow of obscenities and blasphemy was clearly so familiar to Denny that all he said was: "Here we are, so don't repeat yourself, Mother M."

"Mother," snorted Mrs Minchin, "a hard time your mother must have had of it birthing you, with that head on you."

It was true that the sergeant, although short and stocky, had a large long head.

"Come on in with you so that I can get away home when this poor girly has gone. Although I know not when that will be."

"No one to keep her company here then?" asked Major Mearns, looking into the darkness.

"No, not today. No, she has come from nowhere, poor thing, and no one claims her, Not a soul. The gardener that dropped last Sunday went off, and not before time, to be buried yesterday."

Major Mearns put his arm around Mindy to draw her forward. "Just a look, my dear... Lift the cloth over the face, Mrs Minchin if you will, please." He turned back to Mindy. "Don't be nervous, my dear."

"I am not." Which was not true, and all the time she was asking herself why had she been brought here to look at the dead woman. She closed her eyes briefly,

55

then opened them to stare down.

She saw a young face on whose cheeks dark stains were already appearing together with a puffiness. The hair was loose about the face, straight and clotted with dirt.

For a moment, there swum darkness in her eyes, then she took a deep breath.

"No, I do not know her, poor soul."

"Does she look like anyone you know?"

"It is hard to be sure."

"In life, when breathing?"

"Yes," said Mindy slowly. "Like Mrs..." she fumbled for the name. "Like the actress."

"And?" The Major leaned forward. "Come on, now."

"Like my mistress, Miss Burney... that is what you want me to say, isn't it? Yes, there is a likeness."

Mindy stood there, her green shawl draped over her shoulders. She hugged it to her as the two men led her back through the corridors. She heard them murmuring that this dead girl was a mystery   might never be solved. Why was she brought into the Castle? Was she killed there or outside? There were so many ways into this huge building.

In the Major's room, she found herself sitting in the armchair by the fire with her eyes closed.

She heard the Majors voice. "What a Trojan. Get her some brandy, Denny, she deserves it. This is our girl."

—Why am I their girl, thought Mindy, dimly through her sense of confusion induced by the near fainting fit. What is it they want?

Fanny also had her plans for that evening which she had not shared with Charlotte Minden.

Dressed in dark clothes, her head muffled up in silk and muslin, for she wanted to look well, she made her way out of the castle through a side gate which even Mindy did not know of, and which she had learnt of through listening to Mrs Schellenbarter complaining that it was never locked and guarded as it should be.

Nor was it tonight, Fanny through it and hurrying in the moonlight down a winding slope into the town. She was going to the theatre on her own.

She had made the arrangement quietly because a note from James Manston containing a ticket and a playbill of a play in which he believed she would be interested, written, as he said by "my American cousin, Winter Ames." Winter Ames would perform in this play.

Fanny knew that she was behaving in a way young gentlewomen did not behave but she meant to write for the theatre, because that way came fame and money, and therefore she must learn the ways of that world. In fact, she wanted to, because she wanted freedom, freedom from family and the ordered rule of men. You could be respectable and be a woman in the theatre, she thought of Aphra Behn, you did not have to be like the licentious Mrs Robinson... an actress it was true and not a writer.

Fanny knew it was rash, setting out alone for the theatre, when two women had already been murdered, but she knew that it was only the paths nearest to the castle that would be empty. In the town itself there would be plenty of people around on this moonlit night. In any case, it was not yet dark. She closed her mind to the blood in her room, to thoughts of the dead woman, and to the wild visions of last night of a mad and violent King. Such rubbish, she told herself, all would be resolved reasonably.

There was a heady happiness inside her that drove out fear so that she felt confident and strong. But she had taken her precautions: in the reticule that hung from her waist she had a small but nicely sharpened knife. She shut out of her mind the memory of the blood and the knife of last night: Mindy had not come back to her with any message. It must all be some dreadful mistake, she would not think about it now, this was her knife.

Her brother had given it to her before she left home, speaking quietly: "Take this with you, Fannikins, and if you have to go out alone at night... and after all, you are a woman alone, then keep it with you." He had been serious.

Already she could see people walking through the street: there was a plainly dressed woman with a dark shawl and hooked up skirts over a red wincey petticoat, her arm through her husband's who was wearing dark trousers and a checked waistcoat. Behind them sailed a large woman in a big bonnet with a dress, floating with lace. Two bright yellow roses waved from her bonnet.

Not a lady of fashion, Fanny thought, but the wife of a prosperous citizen, a shopkeeper or a lawyer. Yes, there he was, dressed in a smart dark green coat, buttoned over his ample stomach, hurrying up behind her and begging her not to walk so fast.

A bunch of apprentices, surely on their way to the theatre too, were surging behind them, jolly, fresh and young. Fanny delighted in the sight of them.

And there was Mr Manston pushing his way through the crowd towards her. "I was to have called for you. Miss Burney," he said reproachfully, "that was the arrangement in my note."

And I did not mean you should do, Fanny thought, or you might have met Mindy which I did not wish.

"I have a stool for you on the stage so that you will see and hear everything just as well as is possible." He offered his arm which Fanny took, gently, cautiously.

58

"After Mrs Sandys is buried she will have her benefit. For the child and her husband."

There was just a touch of bad taste in this, Fanny thought, even while she let her hand rest on his arm. She had noticed this in James Manston before. Still, one must expect manners to be different with actors, although she felt sure that the young American, Winter Ames, would never offend. His manners were impeccable.

A strange name was Winter, could one be called Summer?

Fanny admitted to herself that she found the company of both men attractive. She was conscious that both men aroused feelings, sensations, actual physical sensations, that she had never felt before. She could not turn away from this because if she wanted to write plays about real women then she must know how they felt.

"I'm glad," she thought.

Truly, she was amazed at her reactions to what had happened to her: the warmth, the dampness. Was she unusual? Why were young women never told? She suspected that Mindy knew more than she did, would not be surprised at these phenomena, but it was better not to ask.

Better? Was it because Mindy was a servant and Fanny herself was a lady? We both have bodies, female bodies.

She let James Manston settle her on a seat on the stage. He bowed and left her. Fanny's neighbour was the woman in the bonnet with flowers hanging from it whom she had observed on the way to the theatre.

"Mrs Cheesman," said the woman, holding out a friendly hand. "And this is my spouse: Joseph Cheesman."

"Miss Burney," said Fanny softly.

"Joe and me come often to the theatre, 'tis our great pleasure. Mr Manston dines with Joe and me on many occasions."

Fanny bowed. She had nothing to say.

"Is it not terrible, the death of the poor young actress? I have laughed many times at her comic performance, and I know she was a particular favourite of Mr Manston." Did her eye droop in a wink? "And he was flummoxed when she said she was off to London to work with Mr Sheridan. But it is best not to dwell on it, my Joseph says, and I agree with him, so I set out to-night in my new bonnet, all set to enjoy myself."

Fanny managed a smile, but still had nothing she could say.

Mrs Cheesman had however: "I can see you and I would be friends, you have just the look of a person that suits me. We should be delighted if you would dine with us too. On the next night when the moon is full? I set a good table, Mr Cheesman being in the business so to speak."

—A butcher, Fanny thought.

"We keep the best Madeira in Windsor."

—A wine merchant, Fanny decided.

"My Joe has three provision shops; two in Windsor and one in Egham; he thinks to open one with his cousin in London, in Piccadilly, no less." Mrs Cheesman laughed happily; "I tell my Joe that I shall be quite a lady of fashion then, for there will be no keeping me from London." She lowered her voice a fraction and spoke behind a cupped hand: "My sister is a milliner to the Court, I may tell you, so I will be dressed point davisee." She lowered her voice still more. "And as you may guess she knows all the stories about the Prince of Wales and Mrs Robinson and Mrs Fitzherbert and all the other ladies... she has a score of stories. She is up to the mark with anything."

Fanny wondered what she meant by that strange phrase, but she was saved from answering by the appearance on stage of Winter Ames to start the Prologue.

The play called *The Mayday Marriage* was a light piece, but well written, Fanny thought, and well performed.

The elegant figure, the pleasing, light voice with deeper undertones of Winter Ames drove away the figure of James Manston who had no part in this play but who had slid into a seat at the end of the row of four, where he sat next to Joseph Cheesman.

Without conscious deliberation, Fanny arranged a table for both men in her mind: Winter Ames, first, James Manston, second.

The audience seemed to agree with her for there was much clapping.

"A handsome feller, now, isn't he, Miss Burney." Mrs Cheesman did not bother to whisper her praise. "He'll get a benefit soon, I trow, Mr Manston is always generous to those he likes. But they are both such taking men, and I don't like Mr Ames less for being American."

Fanny hardly knew how it came about but she found herself agreeing, first to be taken by James Manston, with the Cheesmans in tow, to visit Winter Ames back stage, and then...

"There is a carnival down on Peascod Piece tonight," said Winter Ames, gathering her somehow with her consent or without it, she could not tell which, into a warm embrace.

He had not changed his dress but had removed his wig.

"You must come, we must all go, it is for Mrs Sandys. A collection, you know... James has bought tickets for us all."

"I could do no less," smiled Manston.

Fanny wondered what profit was in it for him, she

had already decided that James usually had more than one motive.

Down on Peascod Piece, the small open patch of land further down the hill from the theatre, there was already the noise of music and laughter. The moon was going behind the clouds but the carnival area was lit by flambeaux. The music came from three violins playing jaunty dances.

"Meant to be like Vauxhall in London," whispered Winter in her ear. "A pleasure garden. If tonight goes well, James will make it regular... Mr Cheesman provides the funds... not the fun," said Winter, looking about him, "he has not much of that to offer, but his wife will do her bit."

She was already dancing, flowers on her bonnet waving to and fro with her vigour.

Fanny stood there while the dancers whirled around her. Some were singing as they moved.

"I have been to Vauxhall, it is not much like it."

"This is not London, it will do for Windsor, do you think?" Fanny thought it would not do for her, already her head began to ache. She could see a line of sedan chars waiting for hire in the dark beyond the ring of flambeaux.

Winter saw her look. "Shall I put you into a chair, Miss Burney, or will you let me walk up the hill?"

Fanny moved a step or two closer to the sedan chairs, each with its pair of sturdy, none too clean, porter men. One of them winked at her, another waved. Fanny thought she would be safer walking unless Winter Ames was to trot beside.

"A ragged set, are they not?" said Winter, "let me offer you my arm in our walk."

Away from Peascod Piece, the night seemed very dark, and their way up to the castle, ran through a narrow alley with small houses on either side. Footsteps were coming up behind them. As they walked up, a crowd of laughing, drunken apprentice came running down towards them, they were driving before them a donkey with a screaming young woman sitting on it.

Fanny stepped aside quickly to avoid the rush; they swarmed through with shouts and jeers. She realised she was separated from Winter.

She stumbled backwards, then an arm stretched out from the door of the house and drew her into it.

FOUR

The hall was dark and very narrow, the figure that was crowded in there with her was tall and thin. Faceless. She could not see a face.

But she could smell breath. Stinking, hot breath. Wet and foul with gin.

She tried to turn away but the hand on her arm still gripped her. She began to scream but a hand was grasped tightly across her mouth. Outside she could hear the shouts and laughter of the apprentice boys who were still rushing up and down the alley. Even if she had shouted no one would have heard her. Fanny felt herself dragged further inside. She managed to slow the progress by digging a heel into the wall, grateful that she was wearing sturdy boots and not light slippers.

It was a man's hand, she never had any doubt of that, and a mighty strong set of fingers. As she dug her heels in while at the same she tried to free her face, she was taking in something of the figure that had grabbed and was dragging at her now.

She wrenched her mouth free. "Let me go, let me go."

No answer, naturally, but a kind of snorting breath above her head.

He was taller than she was, but not much stouter. Thin then, tall and thin. Not the King, then, for he was both stout and tall. This person seemed to be covered by a long, dark cloak. And he smelt, a mixture of smells, some of the body and others, more chemical which she could not give a name to.

"I am Fanny Burney," she managed to get out, still struggling, "Dr Burney's daughter and I am one of the Queen's ladies."

What would that save? The thought darted through her mind, what stupid things we say when are frightened.

She had pushing against her attacker with both hands, but now she was trying to get into her reticule to drag out the knife her brother had given her.

Not much use, giving me a knife, Henry dear, if I am killed without being able to use it. But it was difficult to get into the little bag; she almost dropped it.

A boney set of fingers were back across the mouth, and playing with her lips. Boney fingers and yet the rest of the body pressed into her with its bulk. Fanny bit a finger. There was no cry in response; just that deep noise like an animal growl and the hand was planted back again.

Even as she was struggling her eyes were getting used to the darkness. It was a narrow hall with a room at the end of it, the door was open and some light came from the room.

Some object was hanging up within, perhaps from the ceiling, or even from the doorframe.

But even as she took this sight in, her searching fingers had found her knife. She drew it out and stuck firmly into the arm that held her.

The hand dropped away and Fanny was free. She rushed forward to the door, and even as she did so became aware that a convulsion was taking place inside her, it felt as if her guts were turning themselves inside out.

Oh God, Fanny, the terrible things the body can do to you when you are frightened. What I am learning about myself! In the open air she leaned for a moment against the bricks of the house. The apprentices had gone and there was Winter Ames running down from the top of the alley towards her.

"Fanny, Fanny, where have you been? I thought I had lost you."

"Someone grabbed me in the crowd and pulled me into this house."

"Fanny!"

"But I got away... as you see."

"Are you hurt?" He was staring at her with anxiety.

"No." Her assailant had been, but she did not say so.

"I am going after him. Stay here, Fanny."

"No, Winter, please do not."

But it was no use, Winter Ames was already in the house, she could hear his footsteps.

She still had the knife in her hand which Ames had not noticed, so she slid it back into her bag. Then drew a deep breath, and waited.

He was soon back. "No one there, Fanny. The house is empty. He must have gone out the back door which was unlocked." He put his arm around her. "Lean on me, let me support you. Can you walk? Or shall we go back for a chair?"

Fanny was determined to walk. "I prefer to walk."

Slowly they made their way to the castle gate where the soldier on duty recognised Fanny.

Just as they approached the gate, Winter drew her back:

"Fanny, the man, what did he do to you?"

"Nothing, nothing..."

Winter studied her face. "It was bad enough, but it could have been worse."

Soberly, Fanny said: "I know that... I could have been killed."

Savaged first, Winter thought, then killed.

"Thank God, you got away. I blame myself for losing sight of you."

"The crowd separated us. It was not your fault." He held her hand. "Bless you for saying so. And now... will you be comfortable to walk on alone?"

"Yes," Fanny towards the soldier. "He knows me, and I know him. The castle walks are safe."

I hope so, she thought as she sped through them, oh I hope so!

Winter watched her go, watched till she was out of sight, then turned away.

When she got to her room, she took off her soiled undergarments and got herself to bed. She lay for a long while staring through the bed curtains and the narrow cell like room.

Every so often, she shuddered, she knew she had been near evil.

In the morning, she was awaked by Mindy drawing the bed curtains.

"So where were you, miss? I know you were out, because I brought you a cup of chocolate and there was no sight of you... And since did not drink it then, I have brought you a cup this morning."

Fanny thought of her reticule with the bloody knife in it, and the soiled clothes.

"I went to the play."

"With wicked Mr Manston?"

"He is not so wicked," said Fanny, sipping the hot chocolate.

"Not so very, compared with some," agreed Mindy. "And was the play good?"

"I enjoyed it." But her voice, her eyes, gave her way.

Mindy looked at with a question in her eyes.

"So tell me, miss, what did you not enjoy?"

Then Fanny told her what had happened the night before. Or most of it, but not all, not even then.

Mindy drew her lips together, but there was no mirth in them and her eyes were grave. "You were lucky, miss."

"I had a knife."

"You had a knife," Mindy repeated.

"My brother gave it to me before I left. I took with me..."

"I used it, Mindy."

There was a moment of silence. "And did you kill anyone?"

"No, just a wound."

"I respect you, miss. We should all wound those who attack us."

And then, Fanny told her what she had seen but said nothing of so far. "Mindy, in the light of the candles, I could see something hanging in the room behind."

"A man?"

"No, Mindy, I saw a skeleton."

Mindy helped Fanny dress, then she saw her off on the day's duty with Queen Charlotte. "I shall be gone all day, I wait on the Queen through chapel, then dress her for an audience, they stay with her, Mrs Schellenbarter being ill. Late tonight I shall be free." Mindy curtsied and was silent, nor had Fanny said more about her feelings.

"Miss Burney, ma'am," said Mindy at her most formal. "You and I must go to the Major and speak with him."

—A skeleton, she was thinking.

"I shall be late, I shall be late," cried Fanny, beginning to run.

Mindy was adamantine: "Tonight?"

"Tonight," agreed Fanny over her shoulder. When she got to the Queen's chambers she found all in disorder with the Queen sitting in a chair, crying.

In the room beyond, the royal bedchamber she heard shouting and angry cries. It was the King.

Mad again, she thought.

Confident in her ability to arrange the meeting, that evening Mindy strode through the corridors and staircase, finding her way by memory, to the Major's room. She herself slept on a truckle bed in an upper room, an attic under the roof, cold in winter and hot in summer, but thought she did better than the Major's room in these subterranean quarters.

The Major and Sergeant Denny enjoyed a simple supper together, sent up from the royal kitchens below, followed by a glass port that might, just might, have come from the royal cellars.

"I heard in the kitchens that His Majesty is took bad again," said the Sergeant as he enjoyed his tipple.

"That kitchen maid, how does she get all the gossip?"

"Oh they have ears in the walls, these girls. But to be truthful, she gets it from a footman who was there who told a maid of the bedchamber who told a laundry maid ironing bed sheets who told the kitchen maid. Something like that."

"A long route."

"But true nonetheless."

"You keep your ears close to the wall too, Sergeant."

"That's what you pay me for, Major."

"I don't pay you, Mr Pitt does."

"And where does the money come from?"

The Major supped his port. "From you and me in the

long run, that is always where money from the great ones comes from, and there is none greater than Mr Pitt."

"There is some truth in that," said the Sergeant appraisingly.

Mindy arrived at the Major's rooms where she tapped on the door. As she expected it was answered by the Sergeant.

"Welcome as always, Miss." He bowed low as he let her in.

The Major remained next to the port bottle but he too gave a slight bow. "Something to tell, my dear, this not being a call of politesse."

Mindy wondered where the Major picked up these phrases... from the wars in France? "No." In spite of her desire to appear to appear calm in front of these two men, she could not keep the emotion from her voice. "Miss Burney has been attacked."

Quickly she told them the story of Fanny's adventure.

"A nasty adventure," agreed the Major.

"She might have been killed."

"You think her attacker was the murderer? You may be right." The Major looked at Sergeant Denny. "Your opinion, Denny."

"The Windsor murderer it was, sir," said the Sergeant with military precision. "So I believe."

Major Mearns stood up and paced the room. Action was now the order of the day.

"Tell me again how Miss Burney described her attacker."

"Tall, big hands, thin hands she thought."

"Not the King then," said Sergeant Denny.

Hesitantly, Mindy said: "She could not truthfully say

as to size, the man was shrouded in a great loose robe."
Then she added: "She felt his belly pressing into her."
—Fanny had put it more delicately but Mindy was
blunt.

"We will continue to think about the King, Sergeant."
The Major stood behind Denny and patted on the shoulder. "Other names, other names."

"Almost any of the Poor Knights of Windsor," responded
the Sergeant gloomily. "But since they are mostly drunk I
do not know which one would be up to it."

"Miss Burney was sure her attacker was not drunk."

"Mr Smelt is tall."

"Why the castle? It could be any man from the town
or near," said Mindy sharply. Mr Smelt, who always
spoke to her politely, was a favourite of hers.

The Major and Sergeant Denny exchanged glances.
"We think the castle," said the Major. "We favour it."

"There are all the soldiers," Mindy pointed out.

"We excuse the army," said the Major.

"No, it doesn't sound like a soldier unless he was mad
from too much campaigning."

"No soldier goes mad that way: dead or disabled, yes."
Mindy was thoughtfully, "Besides, Miss Burney thought
her attacker was old."

The Major stopped in his march round the room: "We
must speak to Miss Burney."

"She is in waiting on the Queen all the day because
of Mrs Schellenbarter being ill."

The Major did not like Mrs Schellenbarter: "That
woman, now she is a Prussian soldier in skirts! Could
she be the attacker?"

Mindy opened her mouth to say that Fanny would
certainly know if her attacker had been a woman.

"No," said the Major, before she could speak. "I do
not ask that question."

72

"Better talk to Dr Seaton," said Sergeant Denny. "He knows everything... all the talk comes to him as he goes about doctoring."

"Miss Burney first, then the good doctor," and he laughed. The Sergeant did not.

"Miss Burney may be very late. Sometimes the Queen keeps her till all hours... And if the King is ill... he likes Fanny, he clings to her. Really clings, holds on I mean, and it is hard for her to get away."

"The Queen could help her." There was a question in his voice.

"But what can she do? He is the King after all. The Queen doesn't like it though, Fanny says."

So we have heard, thought the Major.

Distantly, they heard the big castle clock chiming the house. It struck nine times.

Mindy moved towards the door. "I will see if Miss Burney is back."

Sergeant Denny came with her. "I will see you on your way." He walked with her through the lower corridors then up a staircase towards where Fanny had her rooms. Politely, he made to leave Mindy there.

"Wait a minute," he said suddenly, "Who is that?" He held Mindy back.

A tall man was pacing the corridor, his back towards them, pretending to study the portraits of various dead princes and royal dukes. Then he turned round to look their way.

"Nothing wrong," said Mindy, "It is Mr Winter Ames... the actor from the playhouse... he has come to see Miss Burney. He would be wondering how she is and wanting to ask. He is a gentleman."

Sergeant Denny nodded. He had heard of Winter Ames and seen him before.

"I will leave you then."

When he got back to where the Major was sitting by his fire, reading his paper, stood for a moment looking, then poured himself a glass of port.

"I take the liberty," he said.

"Help yourself and thank the King."

"Of course," said Denny, as if thinking aloud. "One could not suspect the Queen of murder."

Major Mearns continued to study his newspaper. "As I may have said before, she is a German princess. And Queens have their ways of dealing with enemies: you can be sure. An honour, a little knighthood, or money, thus will they pay for any service done."

Mindy walked up to Winter Ames; he bowed to her and held out his hand. "Winter Ames, ma'am. You recall? We have met."

Mindy hesitated, then she thought: I am a servant, he is an actor, we both serve. She took his hand and shook it. "Charlotte Minden, Miss Burney's maid. Yes, I remember."

"So you will know how Miss Burney is? How is she? Is she recovered?"

Silly man, Mindy thought, if Fanny had not told me everything, as she might well have been so, not all ladies, indeed precious few are as free with their maids as Miss is with me.

"She is nicely, thank you, sir."

"She told you what happened? I should have looked after her better."

Mindy looked severe but thought with some amusement that Miss Fanny usually did what she wanted however well she disguised it. Growing up with the benevolent despot, Dr Burney, had taught her how to act too.

"Will you tell her that I called? I could not come earlier, rehearsal all the morning, the play tonight... May I come tomorrow?"

"Not for me to say, sir," said Mindy in a prim little voice.

He looked at her with bright blue eyes, a handsome man, she thought. "I will come, I will come."

"You are acting, sir."

"And I think you are acting too, Miss Minden." Laughter is allowed, thought Mindy and she began to laugh. If this is an American, I believe I should like America.

She drew herself up; "Sir, do you live among savages?"

He held out his hand again. "Honours even... I will call tomorrow. And guard your mistress... I do not like the Windsor murderer. Now we do not have them in America."

"You will, you will, they will come in time."

Ames hesitated, then he said: "Is there anyone who is specially interested in Fanny? I do not ask for personal reasons you understand."

Mindy frowned; "She has admirers," she said cautiously. "I was thinking of more than that... is there anyone who watches her, pursues for love or harm?"

Mindy said: "I know what you mean."

"So will you watch?"

"I do already."

In a soft, actorish voice, he said: "There are stories going around the town, hard to believe stories about a certain personage, but many do believe. I will not say more. Perhaps I do not need to?"

"There are stories told in the castle also," said Mindy, keeping her voice expressionless.

"I see we both have the same worries... Have you a name to offer?"

Mindy shook her head.

"I have no name either, Miss Minden, but I have a smell of that person. I went into the house and noticed a smell. Smells describe people sometimes, this was a rich, royal smell." He looked at her with a question in his eyes.

Mindy curtsied, but said nothing. Then: "Kings cause revolutions but they do not kill in person, do they? They send others, I think," she added softly: "Unless it is their pleasure."

"You are a clever woman, Miss Minden." Winter Ames bowed as he said goodbye.

Satisfied with her enjoyable brush with Winter Ames, Mindy went to sit by Fanny's fire to wait for her. She had never met a man like Winter Ames before. Perhaps it was being an American.

Ames walked back down towards the town, nodding his head politely at the guard who had let him pass, and thinking that although it might be that he loved Fanny, with her one did not laugh, but with Charlotte Minden one did. She was clever too, and he valued that in a woman which was not the case with all the men he knew. Perhaps all Englishmen wanted pretty dolls to love. He thought some did, certainly.

Fanny came into the room, her face white and tired. "Such a day, such a day. The King is still ill, or so they say for I never saw nor heard him. He may not be in the castle, perhaps they have sent him away."

"Perhaps he is hidden." Mindy was handing Fanny a dish of tea.

"Kings cannot be hidden," said Fanny. "Or not for long," she sighed and sipped her tea. "No, he is sitting in his great bed in the great bedroom with the bed curtains drawn all round him."

"What does the Queen say?"

"The Queen says nothing to me. I am only a servant, Mindy." —And I am a servant to a servant, thought Mindy, and if you do not choose to talk to me, I must

accept. You are kind to me but if you chose to be un-
kind, then I must accept that also. It was what you want
that must be done. I know my place.

"I have been busy myself today," Mindy said. "Are you
too tired to talk tonight?"

Choosing her words carefully, she told Fanny of her
interview with Major Mearns and Sergeant Denny.
"They can help, they must help. Will you speak to them?
Will you do it tonight?"

"I am so tired."

Mindy was urgent. "Miss, this must be done. There
have been two murders in this town. You have been
followed, you have been attacked, blood has been found
in this room and a knife. This may be the work of a
madman, of a great madman. The Major is set to discover who the killer is."

Fanny shook her head. "Can he do this?"

"He is an honest man, miss. If he cannot, then no one
in this town can and no woman is safe."

"Menace indeed," she got up and paced around the
room. "This is a castle, one is supposed to be safe in a
castle, that is what castles are: places of safety. But
bloody things happen in castles too. Shakespeare knew
that. Think of Macbeth."

"Now don't worry about Shakespeare, miss, we have
enough to do with now."

Fanny put her hand to her head. "Yes, I am very tired,
but take me to Major Mearns."

Mindy wrapped a cloak around Fanny and led her
through the passages with a lighted candle in one hand
and the other holding Fanny's hand.

"Are we going down to the dungeons?"

"There aren't any dungeons any more, miss, they call
them cellars, but no, to the right here, down these stairs.
Watch how you go," as Fanny stumbled slightly.

"There are always horrors in dungeons even if you call them cellars."

You have read too many horror tales, miss, and perhaps you have written one. Or are writing one now.

You wouldn't do that to me, my lady? Play-act the whole thing: attacker, skeleton, blood and knife? No, no.

She tried to think how much she knew of her own knowledge: the watching figure, yes, but what else? She pushed the suspicion away as unworthy. Not my Miss Fanny, no. Never.

Mindy tapped on the Major's door, then without waiting for an answer led Fanny into the smokey room where the two sat on either side of the fire.

They rose and bowed as Mindy introduced Fanny. As she looked from the roughish, burly men to her tired, frail companion who had responded with natural grace and politeness to the two men she saw the difference between them. Fanny, fine boned and delicate, was a lady, she came from a different world.

Now this is a play, she thought, what a confrontation, what a scene with Fanny facing these two men in this dark room with me looking on.

"Miss Burney," she said, "Major Mearns and Sergeant Denny. They want to help you."

"It has been hard to know to whom to talk." Fanny spoke in a soft voice as if she was reluctant to talk even now.

"Miss Minden has told me of your misadventures." He added, in a brooding voice. "In this country it is hard to get things moving fast. Moving at all. Kings have it all their own way. Their own time."

"What is he talking about?" Fanny's eyes asked Mindy, who could only shrug. I am not in the mysteries, her shrug said. It's a No Man's Land into which I can let them go, and you, but I will stay this side of reality.

"But I am in a position to help you. There is one power greater than the King, and that is Parliament, and in Parliament it is, saving all their graces in the Lords, it is the House of Commons and in the Commons, none greater than Mr Pitt." He was all but crossing himself as he went through the litany.

"And Mr Pitt is my protector and hence yours, Miss Burney. Should you be attacked by the great and royal... no names, no names... it his power that will see you right." Sergeant Denny kept silent.

"Now tell me what happened if you will... sit you down comfortably and tell me."

In a docile voice, too tired perhaps to protest Fanny went over what had happened.

"Now let me tot it up," said the Major when she had finished.

"A watcher, you detect a hooded figure, face not seen, several times when the King and Queen, you in attendance, promenade on the castle terrace. A public occasion. This person cannot be identified. Looking at you, you feel."

Fanny nodded, and so did Mindy, with energy.

"Two: you go to the theatre, and feel his presence in the audience."

"I sensed someone," said Fanny. Here Mindy kept quiet because she had sensed nothing. But I am not giving to sensing things, she told herself, that is for gentry.

"Back in your room there traces of blood to be seen and a knife. I have the knife. Washed clean." He looked at Mindy. "An ordinary knife. Many such in the castle."

He added in a deep voice: "I do not forget that an

actress and woman of the town have been brutally murdered."

"The Coroner," Fanny began, but he interrupted her.

"We cannot count on the Coroner, I know James Blandwistle, he will sit on both bodies and pronounce them dead. Thus far and no further. The Magistrate in his turn will get no further, Sir George will leave it to the Coroner, Mr Blandwistle is a good man but not clever."

As you say, thought Mindy, no help there.

"And then you were attacked, Miss Burney. You were separated from your companion, the actor Winter Ames, dragged into a house by a person, a man, who had thin hands but a large belly. You escaped by your own efforts because you had a knife. You saw a skeleton."

Fanny found her voice: "I did," she said in a decided way. "It hung, it dangled, there was a light behind it."

"There is sickness here," went on the Major. "For such situations you need a doctor. I have a doctor."

"Dr Seaton is the name, he will know all the sick of soul and mind as I will know all the rogues and villains... Between us we will put a name to your attacker."

"And to the murderer?"

"If they be one and the same man, yes."

Fanny and Mindy left together and the Major and Sergeant Denny walked a little way with them. Partly for good manners but more because the Major thought you could tell a lot about a woman if you walked by her side. And Fanny puzzled him.

Soon, he bowed them goodbye and he and Denny took an outside path and walked down the grand downward concourse. A lone horseman on a black mare passed them.

"There goes Lord Frederic Bertie, Miss Burney's beau,

or so they say," said Denny. This was not strictly true, or only in so far as he might admire Miss Fanny without Fanny returning the interest. But some devil made Denny say it. Was it jealousy? "A fine nag, he's got."

The Major gave him a quick, dismissive glance. "He rides like a German."

And what worse thing could an English gentleman say?

FIVE

The two young women went back through the corridors together, a flickering candle in Mindy's hand.

"Dr Seaton?" queried Mindy. "Is he the King's doctor?"

"No, the King's physician is a much grander person... I think Dr Seaton attends on the young princesses. I have seen him in the distance on occasion."

"I would like to see him, I trust the Major and Sergeant Denny even more but, they are about their own business in this. They are Mr Pitt's servants, they will help us if it suits him."

"I know where the doctor lives, that is, I know where his house is. Mr Smelt told me, it is at the bottom of Castle Mound Hill. One of the oldest houses in Windsor, Mr Smelt said, perhaps older than the castle itself."

"Tomorrow... today is it already, we will go there," said Mindy with decision.

Fanny was doubtful. "The King has been roaring all day. I don't believe I can leave her Majesty." Would not be allowed to, she meant, there was no freedom in royal service.

"Mrs Schellenbarter knows when to be ill."

"I don't love her, Mindy, as you know well, but I believe she does suffer, and this is why she gets so angry. Pain is the whip." And I am the one she whips, Fanny thought, but did not say so.

They walked on in silence, sometimes stumbling in the shadows.

"I should like to see this Mr Pitt," said Mindy. "Major Mearns talks of him as if he was a god. He is a great man, to be sure."

"He comes to Windsor sometimes. I have seen him in the distance."

"What sort of a man, is he?"

"He has a good manner, you would believe and follow what he said." Then she added, perhaps fatigue had loosened her mind and tongue. "He walks as though he was walking on eggs but does not mind if he breaks them... Of course, he has to walk backwards when he leaves the King."

Mindy laughed, the picture amused her: "The manager of the theatre has to walk backwards when he takes the King to the royal box... and he must carry a great, lighted candelabra... now that would be an egg to break."

Both young women laughed. "Did you drink any of the Major's port, Mindy?" asked Fanny suddenly.

"No, but I feel as if I did." Mindy added, "Mr Pitt... does he bring a wife with him?"

"Oh no, ministers of the King do not brings wives to Windsor. He is not married."

"Prefers young lads, does he?" asked Mindy. "They say in the taverns he does, so my father says."

Fanny thought for a moment of her own father making such a statement to his daughter. If he did, she thought, he would probably pass it off with some comment in Greek about ancient Greek society and make a scholarly thing of it.

In the distance of the long corridor came voices, shouting. It was too dark to see anything but they could feel movement, the air vibrated as if the movement was violent.

Then the noise and movement stopped. The two young women listened.

"Was that... could that be... the King?" Mindy tried to see Fanny's face.

"I don't know."

"I feel as though the walls are drawing in on me." Fanny tried to laugh. "This is not like you, Mindy."

"Even I have my imaginings."

The voices started again, shouts and one voice above all the rest.

It was roaring, roaring.

"It is the King."

They listened, there was no doubt at all, the King was roaring. He was coming closer.

Down the corridor raced a white clad figure, hair streaming, mouth wide. Roaring.

Behind him a valet and the lord in waiting. "Your Majesty, your Majesty," Lord Downside was calling. But the King roared on.

Fanny and Mindy drew against the wall as the King came up to them. He stopped when he saw them, stopped his shouting and said politely: "Good evening, Miss Burney, I hope you find yourself well?"

"Very well, your Majesty," said Fanny with a curtsy.

"No need to curtsy, my dear, no need. It is too late at night for that. You should be in bed, my dear young lady, you should be in bed."

The valet and Lord Downside had caught up with the King but did not seem to know what to do, and stood there silently. The King came up to Fanny and took her hand. "My dear Miss Burney, you must let me advise you, a young lady must protect her complexion, it will never do to be out so late. We talked once before on this subject, my dear, as you may remember and I gave you good advice, as I believe you agreed then..." He was clinging to her hand, his speech getting faster and faster. Soon she could not make out what he was saying.

"Your Majesty," she said, trying to draw her hand away, but the King hung on.

Lord Downside came up, bowed, and said: "Will your Majesty come to bed?"

With a roar, the King was off. Racing down the corridor at full voice.

"Where is the King going?" asked Fanny as the valet and Lord Downside ran after him.

"Who knows," panted the valet. "Out to the Great Park and hunt the deer, I daresay."

Silently Fanny and Mindy continued on their way. Down the staircase, round the corner and to Fanny's rooms.

"And did the King give you good advice at Kew?" asked Mindy as she helped Fanny undress.

"I daresay he did," Fanny answered wearily. "He met me in the gardens, although I tried to hide. But he chased me round the bushes and held on to my hand for ever so long. He talked so fast I could not make out what he said."

"Well, he certainly does go on the rampage," observed Mindy as she brushed Fanny's hair. "But it seems he always has a couple following him... I believe he could break loose though if he wanted and get away on his own, although not in that nightgown, but he seems more anxious to hold a young lady's hand than to cut her throat. Perhaps it goes in seasons with him, one day a killing, next day a touch more gentle."

"He is sick," said Fanny.

"Ay, that he is." Mindy let the brush drop. "So we know what we must do."

Fanny looked at her in query: "Mindy?"

86

"What do you do when you are sick? You call on a doctor. We will call on Dr Seaton."

The Major and Sergeant Denny were both men who slept heavily and well (a due admixture of claret and brandy aiding this) but their life had disciplined them to wake early when necessary.

The day after seeing Fanny and hearing her story, and while Mindy and Miss Burney still slept, the two were breakfasting. Their breakfast was a pint of porter and a slice of beef on bread.

In daylight, or such as penetrated the Major's deep down room, revealed a cosy, untidy scene of bachelor comfort with a high backed chair for the Major and settle facing the fire for the Sergeant. There was always a fire whatever the weather outside. A round table was between them and held the porter and the beef and the bread which the Sergeant cut in hefty slices and held out to the Major on a knife.

"Thank 'ee, thank 'ee." The Major drank deeply, then drew upon his pipe. "We must call upon the magistrate and see the coroner."

Through a mouthful of beef, Sergeant Denny said he doubted if they would talk to them.

"I know Sir George, the Magistrate," said the Major with satisfaction. "A good man."

A good man in the Major's parlance, thought Sergeant with some cynicism, meant a man who kept a good table and a good cellar and was liberal with them. Not such a bad test, he thought.

"And the Magistrate knows the Coroner who will hold the Inquest on both murdered women... his nephew by marriage." The Major swallowed another draft. "Married to his niece, a handsome woman but with the temper of the devil."

"So we call on Sir George?"

"Not without warning, not without something first."
He finished eating and went over to his desk in the window where it was now possible to see what you were reading or writing in a pale band of sunlight. "I will scratch out a little note and you will deliver it."

Scratch was the word, thought Denny when he had the envelope in his hand. Calligraphy was not a great skill with the Major.

He tidied himself, brushed his hat, which had seen many summers, and planted it firmly on the side of his head.

He walked smartly down the castle hill, out of the castle environs, saluting the sentry and making for Sir George's house which was the other side of the river, over the bridge and towards Eton.

A handsome new house of red brick betokened Sir George's prosperity with three basement windows on either side of the steps. "Money from the West Indies," the Major had said. Slaves and sugar, Denny told himself, but we are all slaves one way and another.

Denny climbed the three white steps to the door and pulled the bell which he heard ringing in the distance.

After a paused the door was opened by a stout footman in livery who looked hard at Denny and said: "Tradesmen below." Denny stood his ground. "Not trade. This is a note for your master from Major Mearns; I am to take an answer. I will wait." And he pushed his way inside.

He was left in the hall, from which a centre stairway led upwards; a big double door was on one wall, two doors on the wall facing.

The manservant returned. "This way, Sir George will see you."

The door at the end of the hall was opened and he

went through to a small, book lined room, to find Sir George, fat and bald, warming his back against a fire with a dog at his side. In his hand was the Major's note which he was reading.

All that Sergeant Denny got from him was a nod as he went to his desk to write a reply, which was very short. He handed it to Denny.

"Mearns tells me you will be with him, well, you may both see the dead women, and speak to the Coroner."

Denny bowed.

"But I have no hope we shall get the killer."

Denny thought that a stout old magistrate, living in the comfort and security of his own house, threatened by no one, might accept being hopeless, but that if you were a widow, or woman alone, obliged to go out in the streets on your own, aye, and into the castle itself, you might be allowed to be not so cheerful about it.

"We never have done so far," Sir George added.

"You mean there have been other murders before these two?" "...Sir." Denny added hastily, he could tell that Sir George was one who expected respect from his inferiors and there would no doubt that Sergeant Denny counted as one. —I'd like to let you know about that one day, sir, sir, sir, he thought. Times might change, Sir George, we've seen a revolution in America and one in France, you just think on that.

But not even his expression showed these thoughts as he bowed himself out, awkwardly jostled the footman, apologised profusely and went away smiling. "He'll feel that foot for some time after I trod on it." He knew the weight of his own boots.

"I don't see Sir George as kindly as the Major does," he told himself as he walked away. "But the Major, for all his jokes, is an authority man, I am not, I am for equality," and then he added with an inner laugh, because he was a man of humour, "for myself if not others."

Back in the castle he found the Major smoking his pipe and reading a copy of the London *Times*. Yesterday's *Times*, since it took several hours for the paper to arrive in Windsor. This paper had already been read by at least one other person judging by the state of the pages.

Kippered, thought Denny. Like my officer.

"Nice lot of murders in London," he said, reading what he could see in the back of the paper.

"They get all over the place," the Major spoke absently. "Nasty to-do in Parliament, this one shouting at this one and the other bellowing back. Fine gentlemen."

"Still, we will never have a revolution in this country while they can all shout at each."

"If there is a revolution," said the Major, suddenly waking up. "I know which side you will be on."

"I wouldn't be for beheading the King, he's not a bad old boy when in his right mind, but I would sentence him to evening after evening at a Shakespeare play... Purgatory, for him."

And I know which side you will be on, my dear master, the side that wins.

"Well, do we see the bodies?"

"We do."

"A small victory then."

Sergeant Denny bowed his head.

Talking of winning, he said: "I wonder what your young ladies will do?"

The young ladies, so called, for Fanny was beginning to think being genteel was no bargain while Mindy was realising that between her and her mistress was not so much difference. Mindy knew she was bolder, possibly braver, because Fanny was still burdened with the notion that ladies were timid and easily frightened. But Fanny could be brave when she had to be. Mindy respected her for that. What Fanny could not be was honest about what she felt, and that Mindy did not respect her for.

Or was she wrong? The two young women were on their way to call on Dr Seaton, the evening was misty and quiet, but they preferred it so on this particular mission. Then Fanny said:

"Mindy, did you ever do anything of which you were ashamed?"

Mindy considered: the lies she had told; the day she stole a penny from her old master's purse (a mean man, he owed it to her), that which she had done with at least one man, and not much short of it with another, the various fudges and deceptions, the pushes and shoves and downright nastiness she had fallen into. All had seemed either necessary or desirable at the time.

"Yes," she said. "Now and then I have. Sometimes you just find yourself doing them."

"And does it cause you pain when you think of them?"

"Better not to think." But sometimes in the middle of the nights, one or two scenes did come back to you. Like the time she stole a penny from a blind sailor's begging bowl, even though she knew he was not blind and that the only reason he did not see her was that he was drunk. Blind drunk. Still, not a memory she liked even though he was fat and she was hungry. Very hungry and aged six, that matters more than honour. On the other hand, the memory of the session with old Mrs Henty on how to avoid becoming what Mrs H (also dead drunk) called 'bun heavy' by the insertion of a wad of softened up vegetable leaves up what Mrs H poetically called 'the lover's entrance'. This was valuable instruction which any young girl needed to know, and to remember that if it failed, Mrs H had other suggestions to offer. She was drunk and Mindy had helped her home to her garret in Washleather Lane which was why she got this lesson free. "And always remove the vegetable plug," Mrs H had advised, "or it will stink. But not for six hours."

Mindy remembered all this with a blink and a blush but, on consideration, was not ashamed.

Now Miss Burney certainly had no such memories to make her feel guilty, for ladies did not, but Mindy reflected that guilt and usefulness seemed to go hand in hand.

"You have done nothing to be ashamed of, miss," she said stoutly.

Fanny sighed. "I have nothing much to confess, that is true, but." what the 'but' meant she kept to herself but Mindy knew.

—You have had such stirrings for a man as surprised you, she thought sagely and I could name that man.

"The thing about feeling ashamed," observed Mindy, "is that you go on remembering it but the pain soon fades," wondering if she should pass on to Miss Burney some of old Mother Henty's earthy advice. Winter Ames and James Manston, these are the two men, and of the two it is Manston you chose but it should be Winter Ames.

"I think I might be ashamed of going to see Dr Seaton."

"We must talk to him, ma'am."

"And say we know the King is mad but do you think he is a killer? And what will he answer, but No, Miss Burney, I cannot think my sovereign is a killer."

"Yes, he will say that, but we shall be able to tell if he means it."

They were walking fast, Mindy at her mistress's right

hand, she pulled at Fanny's wrap to slow her down.

"Major Mearns says the doctor knows all the sick of mind and mad in Windsor and that he and Denny know all the wicked so that if any name comes forward twice that is like to be the killer."

Fanny stood still for a moment. Ahead of them, at the bottom of the hill, near to the bridge to Eton, was a dark, low old house with flambeaux on either side of the door. They were smouldering rather than burning which made everything seem even darker.

"Here is the doctor's house. Not such a walk, after all." The castle and the theatre were behind them and the river ahead. On the other side of the hill, newly paved, with a small terrace of houses just being erected, the night watchman was pacing, calling the hours.

"Ten o'clock and all's well." He had a deep and not particularly pleasant voice but each word was audible.

"All's well?" said Mindy. "And two women dead, murdered... I wonder what would count as a disaster? A revolution, or the King being killed?"

She stopped; somehow the King who might be killed in a revolution or fall from his horse seemed to have nothing to do with the old gentleman rushing through the corridors of the castle in his nightgown.

There were no lights to be seen in Dr Seaton's house but that was not surprising, the odd flickering candle cast no great illumination.

Fanny pulled the bell handle in the wall next to the door. She heard it ring, sonorously, distantly, in the house. But no one came. She tried again.

"Bang on the door," said Mindy, seizing the iron knocker. "This is a doctor's house, they must be used to people calling at all hours."

This time she put her ear to the door. "I hear someone coming."

The door was opened very slowly and a face peered round the door. Not a friendly face, a hostile, reluctant face, with small spectacles and a lank stretch of grey hair scragged back making it minimally female.

"Miss Burney wishes to see Dr Seaton," said Mindy firmly. There was no answer. Thin lips remained closed, although the eyes behind the glasses observed Mindy and Fanny sharply.

"From the castle," said Mindy in a firm voice.

The door opened a further crack, but no further.

A voice behind called out:

"Let the young ladies in, Mrs Crook."

"If that is your wish, Dr Seaton."

"It is, Mrs Crook."

Mrs Crook gave a bob to her master who could now be seen behind her and opened the door wider.

Just wide enough for Fanny and Mindy to slide through. A woman of infinite meanness was Mrs Crook even in her opening of doors.

Dr Seaton came forward, hand outstretched. "Miss Burney, I have read your novel and admire it greatly. *Evelina* is a fine work."

"Thank you, sir." Fanny felt his hard, dry grasp. The doctor was a tall, very thin man, with a mane of dark hair so thick and lustrous it looked false.

"Come in, you want to see me? You are not sick, I hope? You know my trade is with the mentally sick." He was leading the way down a long narrow corridor, lined on either side with closed doors. Four of them, two to a side. At the end of the corridor was a room, well lit and with the flicker of a fire in the looking glass on the wall.

Mindy followed behind. She was invisible and accepted it. She walked carefully, slowly. She sensed movement behind those closed doors.

"No, not sick," said Fanny carefully, "But I want to talk to you about sickness."

The room they entered was warm with a generous fire. There was a comfortable red carpet on the floor with a set of handsome chairs about it. Pictures on the walls and that handsome looking glass in the gilt frame. Candles shone here and there, lighting the room.

The doctor motioned Fanny to one. "Sit down, I beg you, Miss Burney."

Fanny sat in a large, well polished oak chair, while Mindy, offered no chair and expecting none, took up her place behind her.

Dr Seaton sat down himself opposite Fanny. "Some wine, my dear Miss?"

Fanny refused politely. She would not take any.

"This is not where I see my patients, they come and go by a different door at the side, poor things."

"I am sorry you see so many locked doors around you, but you can understand that with my patients, it is wise to have all doors fastened."

"You mean some live with you?" Fanny looked around her nervously.

"Just one or two."

Deliberately, Fanny said, but with an innocent air: "But is that safe?"

"Not in the least. Sometimes a little noisy, poor souls, but we soon quieten them with a dose or two of soothing syrup. And those poor creatures who get somewhat obstreperous... we have ways of controlling them... For their own good, you understand, Miss Burney, for their own good."

Tie them to a wooden rack, or fasten their arms behind them in a shroud, thought Mindy. She had a natural cynicism about doctors but little or no experience of them. In the world from which she came the old woman down the road helped you into the world if you were lucky and laid you out when you left it. Otherwise you got on with life on your own.

"But you have a problem?" Dr Seaton put on a pair of gold rimmed spectacles the better to stare at Fanny. "You want to ask me about it?"

Fanny looked down at her hands. "I am worried about a person with whom..." she hesitated, before saying, "with whom I work."

True enough, thought Mindy. In a way. She is clever with words is my lady.

"This person is..." Again she paused. "Agitated."

"Excessively so?"

Mindy caught Fanny's eye, and both remembered the raving, shouting man who had careered down the castle corridors.

"Yes," said Fanny.

"Needing restraint?"

Fanny nodded. "Sometimes a great deal."

"Unpredictable?"

"Yes, and sometimes hard to understand. A good person, you understand, but." Then she plunged into what she wanted to say. "Could such a person kill?"

The doctor rose to his feet and paced round the table. "Unpredictable, violent? I fear so. This person is mad." He approached Fanny, faced her sternly. "But I cannot offer a serious opinion with seeing the person. Then I can make a study and give a judgement."

"I can't bring the person," she added quickly: "I am not responsible for this person... I ask because I wanted to know."

"Why so?"

"There have been two murders in this town."

Dr Seaton's large grey eyes, pale and lucent, stared hard at Fanny.

"You think this person is a murderer?"

Fanny bowed her head but did not answer. Mindy however kept her eyes on the doctor whose face looked pleased. "He knows who Fanny means," she told herself. "Has come to the same conclusion himself, perhaps."

"Why do you come to me, missy?"

"I was told you knew or knew of all the sick and darkest souls in this town."

The doctor began to pace the room, first in silence, then nodding his head. "True, true, so I do." He gave Fanny a sharp glance. "But I am not to give you their names."

Fanny said: "But who would ask? But a murderer, you know, cannot go unpunished."

"I know that the body can be the home of evil as well as the site of the soul," he said in a quiet voice.

He took another turn around the room. "Now, my dear, I have decided; I shall help you. Bring me some hair from your person's head, some cutting from the nails and a handkerchief that has been used..." He looked up at Fanny with a smile. "You see I do not say man or woman... Bring me what I ask for and I will read what these samples can tell me. The body can speak for itself." He continued seriously: "Medicine has greatly advanced, Miss Burney, we have syrups and pills and powders to drive out the poisons from the body and brain. Ethiops mineral, calomel, oxymel of squills... a potent syrup indeed. I do not scruple to say that I have been one of the first to make use of them for the benefit of my patients... I prepare them myself to be sure of their purity, they are not medicines to buy on the street or off a tray in the theatre where one might find anything offered." He held out his hand. "No charge, I do it out of interest."

Fanny rose. "Thank you."

They were led once again through the dim corridor with its closed doors to the front door.

—Behind those doors, Fanny thought, were souls in torment. Mindy hung about trying to listen, she thought she picked up creakings and sighs, but who could tell? No doubt a house like this had rats aplenty.

As they stepped through the door, Dr Seaton took Fanny's hand. "Take care, Miss Burney." Then he pulled her back to give a sibillant whisper in her ear. "When the person shouts and raves, listen to what is said, Listen very carefully for the ravings will tell us much of the illness and its cause. Possibly its cure." Then he lowered his voice a tone more: "In such sickness, the passions rise high, miss. Take heed of their force." He released and drew back to let the two young women depart.

The door banged behind them.

They were out in the streets with a thin rain falling. As they walked through the wet back to the castle, Mindy said: "He knew you meant the King."

"I think so," said Fanny, "and he told me to be careful."

"What did he whisper to you as we left."

"He asked me to listen to the ravings and take notice of the words." Fanny shrugged. "I may not see the King soon, he is off to Kew, I believe where he may rage and swear more freely."

Back in Fanny's rooms after a silent walk through the rain to the castle, Mindy said:

"How will you get the cuttings of the hair and nails?"

Fanny considered; it was not going to be easily done. "I might speak to the King's valet if I could think of the right excuse."

"Have you in the dungeon for being a witch...
Wouldn't burn you these days but you might get hung."
Mindy was not joking, nor did Fanny laugh.

Mindy went on: "No, leave it to me, miss. I shall find
what I want in the sculleries and wash places and priv-
ies where the valets throw out the waste for the night
soil men to collect. They are not choosy where they drop
their waste, those men. It's all bow and scrape and as
Your Majesty pleases but when they get outside it's let
get rid of the old man's shit and throw out his dirty
water... I daresay I could get some of his own water if I
tried... now that might be useful to Dr Seaton, you can
tell a lot from the colour and cloudiness of the piss."

The next day was a wearisome one for Fanny since Mrs
Schellenbarter was still indulging herself in her illness
and keeping to her bed. This meant that upon Fanny
and one maidservant fell the duties of getting the Queen
into her gowns and then settling her wig upon her head.
No easy task, since the Queen, although usually mild
and gentle, reserved for herself the right to be irritable
when she chose about the set of her gown. She was an
awkward shape and size, naturally so after so many
pregnancies, which not even all the whale boning and
lacing could control. This more personal part of her
dressing was performed in an inner room by her personal attendant, Fanny not concerned with it, only with
the nice adjustment of stiff silks, and fine lace, which
was not always easy. Nor was the settling of the wig
simple or comfortable matter since it had to be powdered and although all, including Fanny, put on a white
cotton over-gown, they all of them took on board a great
deal of white powder.

"An odious business, this powdering," thought Fanny
as she scuttled through the corridors back to her own

rooms. "It is out of fashion more and more except at Court."

She was glad to see a fire burning brightly in the grate and the teakettle swinging on the trivet above the flames. She could relax, since the Queen dined alone with the Prince of Wales tonight. Matters too private to be discussed before others, but of course, the whole Castle knew that the question of the Regency was what they would talk about. Mr Pitt was arriving later.

The King was ill, confined to his room, but those passing by in the corridor could hear his voice. They could hear what he said. Not talk you expected from a King.

Mindy hurried into the room. "And did you get talk with His Majesty?" she began to make the tea. Mistress looked so spent and tired that she might drop a little brandy or rum in the cup as she poured it. She would enjoy it herself.

Fanny said no, she had not seen the King, although she had heard him roaring. "I believe the Court might be off to the palace at Kew. The doctors think it will be easier for the King to be nursed there."

"Or tied up like a sausage." Mindy mashed the tea. "Well, I have done better for you and Dr Seaton," she held out a cup. "Take your tea and I will tell you."

Fanny took the cup gratefully, she knew she did not stand up to work as well as Mindy who looked bright eyed and cheerful and was rattling on.

"Mind you, Miss Fanny, it was hard work, I had to jest and play games with the valets and the manservant down below." Better not to tell Miss Burney the nature of the jokes and romps. "But I got some hair from the beard after the barber was done and a sliver of nail from the right big toe. There was something wrong there, so the surgeons were at work on it."

She took a drink of tea, before bursting out with her

news, she tried to sound calm but it was really so startling and interesting. "And I have a jar of his water... Miss, it is, blue. His water is bright blue... purple even... purple for the King."

Fanny frowned as she drank her tea.

"Do Kings always pass purple water, miss?"

"Don't make wicked jokes, Mindy."

"No joke, miss." Mindy was properly humble.

"And where are these..." Fanny sought for a word. "Specimens, where are they?"

"In a basket lent me by one of the gardeners, he uses it for strawberries but I daresay he won't do it again. The basket is locked in a cupboard and I have the key," she drew it from her bodice where she had hidden it. "And I think the basket ought to go down to the doctor, the jar full is not a wine to improve with keeping."

"Yes, I will take them at the first opportunity, but I can't say when that will be... Mrs Schellenbarter may still be laid up."

"What's the matter with her?"

Fanny sighed. "Oh the tiresome French lady is making a long and painful visit. She usually does, I believe."

Mindy was not sympathetic. "She should not eat so well and drink so much red wine, then she would not bleed so strongly. It's only rich ladies that can afford to have the French lady come every month, where I come from women do not bleed so much. Poor feeding and hard work dries them up."

She stopped speaking, she had gone too far, Fanny who was usually so easy with her had held up a hand. "Mind what you say, Mindy."

"Never outside this room, miss," said Mindy with a virtuous air. In a way, this was true, totally loyal to Miss Burney no word about Fanny and her doings ever passed her lips but about others she would gossip as it amused her. On all sides stories floated around, added to, growing all the time. The whole castle was a great echoing chamber of gossip.

Mindy knew so much more of the dark and dirty world than Fanny. Fanny knew this and did not recoil, knowledge was knowledge, she admitted to herself that although she would not have wanted to set foot in this world herself, who knew what life would bring her to? It might be as well to be armed against it.

Women needed to know, sheltering them from the hard truths and the sordid, sad ways of men and women together was stupid. She could never have talked of all this to her parent. What did her mother make of being a woman? She had never spoken beyond the usual platitudes about seemliness and womanly modesty. But her mother had married and borne children. Not total modesty there, then.

Also, although she kept this thought deep inside her, life in the world that Mindy knew seemed freer and funnier, with all its terrors, than the world that Fanny had been brought up in.

She was aware that she had changed since to coming to Windsor and was now prepared to think openly thoughts she had kept underground when she had written *Evelina*.

Was it due to her close contact with Mindy? She could talk to Mindy, sometimes in a kind of code, it had to be admitted, but they understood each other. No stupid ladyish modesty about Mindy but womanly good manners. Yes, Mindy was a woman to respect.

Was it Mindy who had given her this new freedom, or was it the new friendship with the American actor? She thought about him more than she wished. It seemed simple when in the company of Winter Ames to have a free and easy friendship with a man, but when they were apart, she succumbed to the rules she had been taught.

She liked his company, and today, a short, unsigned note had been put into her hand by a footman. "For you, miss."

Fanny read: "Come tonight if you can, alone."

It was not signed, except for a scribble hard to make out, but no doubt in the theatre world, people were casual. She folded and put it in her pocket, but not before she had scribbled a reply and given it to a footman to deliver.

"To the theatre," she said to him, blushing as she did so.

I am a coward, she thought, a prudent coward, because Sophy Todd and Miss Sandys had been free and active, not kept to the rules of genteel behaviour and they were dead. One a prostitute, a lady of the town, and the other an actress, a lady of the stage, true, a wife and good mother, but just on the edge of the protected world, and not all she should be. Easy victims, both?

But Mindy was waiting for an answer. "So what, miss?"

"I will take your basket and your jar of human water down to the Doctor," she said.

"Good, miss, good. If the King is in a way to be a killer we need to know."

If he is a killer, then it will be of women, Fanny thought. She knew what words the King shouted when in his fit; she knew what moved his mind. He shouted obscenities, he complained of the Queen, he made lewd jokes and suggested the fantastic couplings he fancied. Man and beast, woman and child, upright, upside down and inside out were not to be spared.

The doctors and valets listened and bent their heads, tongues still. But they talked afterwards. Even Mr Smelt, the kindest of the King's gentleman spoke of it. "The poor K   ing must be shut up or we will have a revolution," he had said in Fanny's hearing.

"I'll come too, miss."

"No, Mindy. You can't. I have no permission to be away from the castle, so you must stay and if anyone comes looking for me, most particularly a message from the Queen to call me to duty, then you must say I am ill."

"Not very easy if you aren't there to be looked at."

"No one will come into my bedchamber if you are on guard."

"How will you go, miss?"

"I will walk, Charlotte Minden, as I usually do." Mindy seemed surprised I could take independent action.

"I should be with you, miss. It is my job to be with you."

Fanny ignored this. "These slippers will not do for the walk, get me my boots. There, help me on with them... thank you, Mindy."

Oh I am back to Mindy, am I, thought the maid. "Here is your mantle, miss, and your bonnet."

"No, a shawl, just a shawl, the dark one you wear yourself."

Oh, so you are going in disguise, miss, are you, pretending to be me? But I will shake you out of that. "Oh miss, remember how like you are to Miss Sandys. And how she died."

For a moment, Fanny was checked, she stood at the door. "Mindy, I am more at risk in the castle than ever I shall be in the streets of Windsor. The King likes me, Mindy, more than he should and in a way he should not, he reaches out to me. Do you understand what I am saying?" Then Fanny drew the door open, and was gone.

She knew why she was going, and where, after she had delivered the specimens to the good doctor.

"There she goes," said Major Mearns, standing in his door and looking out across the lower courtyard. "Silly girl."

Sergeant came across to see what he could see.

"It looks like Charlotte Minden, that is her shawl."

"But not her walk. No, that is Miss Burney."

"Where is she off to?"

"Not to see her lover, dressed like that. No, the doctor, the great Dr Seaton." There was satisfaction in the Major's voice.

"You sent her off on that trip." It was close to an accusation.

"No, not sent. Encouraged. But she is the only one who can do our business with the doctor. He would not see me."

And quite right too, thought the sergeant, aware that he was never told all that was in the Major's mind, and sometimes glad not to be so knowledgeable.

Fanny arrived at Dr Seaton's, no one had noticed her passage through the street, she was as anonymous as a mouse.

She went to the back door and pulled on the bell. There was a long pause, so long she thought she could have gone to the big front door, Then there were footsteps. The door opened, and there was the doctor.

"My dear young lady, my dear Miss Fanny, you have come alone, as I asked."

SIX

Fanny found she was very close to the doctor, who had come forward to greet her, so near that she could smell the brandy on his breath, Another smell beneath it, as if he had taken some drug. He seemed to sway.

"Are you unwell, sir?" she asked timidly, annoyed at the same time with herself for her timidity. It was hard when you had determined to be a woman of independence, brave and free, to find nervousness creeping over you. But the truth was that she had never before come into contact with a man like Dr Seaton.

But Dr Seaton was larger and taller than she had remembered and he smiled with more strength and enthusiasm than she had noticed before, and which, somehow, did not please her. One should be pleased with smiles and a welcome but somehow she was not pleased.

And then there was his appearance. Was this how one dressed to receive a lady?

Fanny was beginning to understand what a sheltered life she had led. One which had not prepared her for all aspects of Dr Seaton.

He was wearing a richly embroidered silk robe with a fur collar and fun on the sleeves. It fell to the ground, just revealing the tips of embroidered slippers. There was no doubt his appearance was elegant but slightly surprising also. Moreover, he had taken off his wig to reveal a bald pate, lightly fringed with grey hair.

"Not unwell, my dear, and all the better for seeing you. Come you in, come you into the warm and dry." He was opening the door and ushering her in to the hall. "I see you are wearing a shawl... too dark and old for your prettiness, my dear. I took you for your little maid until I saw your face."

—So you were looking out of the window, thought Fanny. I was sure I observed the curtain move.

He took her into a room she had not seen before, a small, comfortable room with a big chair covered in leather, it stood before a brightly burning wood fire. Beside the chair, was a small table on which stood a decanter and a glass, with two calf bound books beside it.

"My evening reading," said the doctor. "I see you have a basket?" He held out his hand. "Give it here." He did not sound so scholarly and gentlemanly as on the last visit, as if a rougher background was showing itself.

He held out his hand.

Fanny nodded, struggling to regain her composure. She felt repugnance and now guilt for what she was doing. These were bits and pieces of the poor old King's body that she was handing over. Mad, he might be, guilty of murder, he might be, but sick he certainly was.

The doctor extracted the small wrapped bundles, sat down, put them on his lap, and settled down to examine them.

"Hair... from the beard, I conjecture, since they are wiry and grey." He picked out a strand of hair. "And this is from the head, since it is longer and softer." The amounts were small, but Mindy had done her best. "Nail cuttings... Not much perhaps to be learnt from such shreds, but useful."

Then he unwrapped the bottle of the King's water which shone like a purple jewel in the candlelight.

"Ah," he held flask up in a kind of triumph. "I have seen this before. This tells a lot."

"Perhaps the colour comes from medicine his doctors give the King," said Fanny nervously.

"No, it is the mortal body itself speaking of its sickness. Poor soul, poor soul, he is ill indeed. Mightily ill. I pity him."

He spoke of pity, but Fanny thought there was more of excitement and pleasure in his voice.

"Is he mad?" Fanny asked. "In your opinion, Dr Seaton, is the King mad?"

"Do you hear him raving and shouting?"

Fanny nodded. She could not deny it. All the castle could hear the King roaring.

"Does he show violence?"

"Sometimes, His Majesty does." Almost all the time, but she flinched from saying so about a man kind when he was not roaring obscenities into the air, and decrying the Queen's virtue. She called him His Majesty as a kind of courtesy as if they were meeting in a corridor of the Long Gallery. He was indeed Majesty, born of a line of Kings. "Yes, they say he can be violent." They? she thought, they? Who are they? I can speak of it myself. When he pressed me to him and would not let me go, I thought I should never escape.

Perhaps Miss Sandys and that other poor creature did not escape?

Unbidden, the thought came into her mind that the woman of the streets had been brought into the castle for the King. For him to make use of.

But who would do that service for him? None of his gentlemen, but perhaps a valet? No, a servant would never be entrusted with such a task. The Major and

Sergeant Denny then? She liked them both but what they were doing in the castle had puzzled her. You could not call them courtiers or servants.

They were soldiers and soldiers and it was acknowledged that soldiers took a different view of matters of sexual relations. They were used to violence and taking what you wanted because tomorrow you might be dead.

As if reading her thoughts, the doctor said: "And of what goes on between men and women, does the King speak of it?"

—Speak, Fanny thought, shout rather, harangue, laugh and spit and offer up lewd imaginings.

Fanny already knew that the salient feature of the King's illness, apart from a show of violence, was talking very fast, incoherently and imprudently.

And this imprudence consisted of a rush of sex talk.

"He shows disgust of the Queen?"

Fanny said she thought so.

"And he is spiteful of other ladies he has loved."

Again Fanny was obliged to say yes, it was so.

"Alas, it shows the man underneath the King, We all have a man underneath that we do not care to own."

He was leaning very close to her, so that Fanny was forced to draw back.

"You are distressed, Miss Burney. I understand. Some wine, take some wine."

Dr Seaton poured out a full glass full of claret.

"No, I thank you."

But the glass was put into her hand with an order. "Sip, just one sip, it will restore you."

"The King is sick, he has a grave illness, but the mind and its dangerous obsessions... I call them dangerous, Miss Fanny because they spring from a misunderstanding of the nature of men and women. He does not un-

110

derstand what the marriage relationship is, what a man and a woman should be to each other, he does not allow for animal nature... Hence he shows disgust and anger..."

The doctor rose and went to his bookshelves to look, walking along the shelves, muttering to himself. "Now where is that book, where is Venette?" But it was only a pretence, Fanny thought, because he had the book on the table by him, and came back and lifted it. "Ah here, here it is. Venette's *Tableu de l'Amour conjugal.*"

The wine glass was taken away, the book was opened on her lap.

Fanny saw at once that it was a manual with advice, anatomies and amorous illustrations. She looked up; the doctor had his face close to hers and was studying her features.

"There is a science here... we must take the King through all this as well as curing his physical state. The mind, Miss Fanny, has great powers of its own to make sick."

Fanny closed the book carefully, thinking that a King who had been married all these years and had so many children perhaps did not need so much instruction.

She found she was both curious to look at the book, and shrunk from doing so. She handed the book back. "Thank you, sir."

Her mouth suddenly dry, she swallowed some more wine.

"There are other aspects of the subject with which the book does not dwell," went on the doctor, his voice gaining weight and enthusiasm. "You must let me show you my specimen tray..." He rose.

"Thank you, no, sir," said Fanny hastily. "I think you are carried away by your subject."

Humming gently with an occasional chuckle, the doctor went to the cabinet on the wall and drew out a tray which he carried back to show Fanny.

"Now here, miss, we have several efficient contraceptive devices..." He let his finger lightly touch the first. "Now here is a sponge, small you see, to be inserted at the proper time." He nodded. "Soaked first in brandy or vinegar." He pointed to a bottle. "Now here is a prophylactic potion... spermicidal or an arbortifaciant." He drew his lips down gravely. "You understand that I am obliged to know of these things, and on occasion, to pass on my knowledge." His voice dropped as he went on and seemed to recede into the distance, for which Fanny was grateful.

Her eyes closed. Distantly, she thought she heard the doctor talking to her, his voice soft and ever softer.

Back in the castle, Mindy kept the fire going and waited for Fanny to return. "She's in no hurry," she thought. Although Fanny thought she had kept her secret, Mindy had guessed that part of Fanny's wish to go on her own involved Winter Ames, a handsome, and taking man whom Mindy too appreciated. But perhaps she preferred a man of action like Sergeant Denny.

This week there was no performances of tragedies or romances at the theatre because a group of comic actors, jugglers and dancers was coming from London to perform. This happened once or twice a year which pleased the lower citizens of the town.

Mindy was prepared to go and enjoy such a show herself, she liked to laugh, but she admired Winter Ames more.

She yawned while wondering what the hour was. She must have been asleep when the castle clock last rang out.

To her surprise, there was a rap on the door. For a

second, she debated ignoring it, then she went forward.

"Who is there?" she called cautiously, before opening it.

"Winter Ames."

Think of the devil, I was just admiring your looks, sir. But she did not say this aloud, instead, still cautious, she opened the door a crack.

There was Winter Ames himself. He paused for a moment as if debating what to say and then: "Miss Burney? May I speak to Miss Burney?"

It was Mindy's turn to debate what to say. Ah well, it had to be the truth, which sometimes, although not always in her experience, was best. "My mistress is not here."

Winter Ames paced the room, then finally came out with: "I had a note from her this evening, delivered by a lad from the castle, saying she would meet me as I had asked."

"Oh," pondered Mindy. —She never told me that, she thought, but whoever does tell the truth about what goes on between a woman and a man. Still, not like my mistress. Also she wondered how Winter Ames has got past the guards at the castle entrance. At night it was not an easy task to get into the castle without a letter of admittance. There were ways, known to the Household.

"How did you get in, sir?"

Winter Ames said briefly:

"I told the man at the gate, I had come to see Lord Vickers... he knows we are friends. His lordship will not mind... I had waited in the theatre, but Miss Burney did not come."

Mindy turned various thoughts over in her mind before coming to no helpful conclusion.

"But I had not asked... She had no message from me."

"She left here on an errand to Dr Seaton," admitted Mindy. "She had an errand for him. I suppose she meant to go to you after." Now I know why she wore my shawl and hood, the artful creature, so she would not look like Miss Burney.

"Seaton? I know the man, or at least, I have seen him." Winter Ames was frowning.

Mindy felt an obligation to explain her mistress's mission, although his dark frown was pleasing, and for herself she had not objection to letting him frown on, as he looked so handsome and manly. She had always like a manly man.

"My mistress had some... samples... to take to Dr Seaton."

Winter Ames was still frowning. Delightful to look at, Mindy thought, but he should not get too angry. He began to walk about the room. Unasked, but that was a man's way, Mindy thought. When anxious, use your legs. One way and another.

But her eyes followed him admiringly. There was no doubt that a jacket of fine cloth, well tailored about the shoulders, with soft linen at neck and wrist, was pleasurable to watch. He was a fine figure of a man.

"I could bed him myself," she thought, "but for my dear mistress, for I do think she loves him." It was a recognised truth that the master could make love to the maid and no one the worse for it (provided care had been taken in the performance thereof) but Mindy knew that her mistress was made of different stuff. And turning a blind eye was not part of her.

"Miss Burney will be back soon," Mindy said. Surely? she thought. What is she doing? The thought of doing anything with Dr Seaton was not to be admitted to the sane mind.

There was silence from Ames.

"How does the troupe from London do?" Mindy asked, to keep the conversation moving, although she already knew they were not doing well.

"Poor," he said briefly, "the best singer fell ill and went back to London, and several others look sickly," said Ames. "A mistake to have them here."

Suddenly Winter Ames swung round. "I am going to look for her. This is a town in which two young women have been murdered."

His stern tone gave Mindy a shiver; not entirely unpleasurable she had to admit.

"I'll come with you."

"No, stay here, in case your mistress comes back."

Mindy accepted what he said, yes, she had to be here for Fanny. She went back to sit by the fire. Yes, he had done his work well, she was now worried about Fanny Burney.

Winter Ames walked quickly through the castle corridors, and out past the guard at the gate, who saluted.

He hurried down the hill. It was now very dark, as the moon had gone down. Windsor was at no time a well lit town.

At the bottom of the hill, he saw a figure crawling slowly towards him. Something in the walk, the tilt of the head, made him hurry on.

"Fanny... Miss Burney."

Fanny looked up dreamily. "I am coming to see you. You asked me and I said I would." Then she paused. "But I misremember... the note was not from you, but from Dr Seaton."

Winter Ames stood still, hesitant. "It's late. I must see you home, Miss Burney."

"Is it late?" Fanny sounded puzzled. "I did not realise... Dr Seaton was showing me," she paused. What had he been showing her? "Medical matters," she said slowly.

Puzzled by her dreamy look, but unwilling to be intrusive, Ames led the way back up the hill. Fanny walked beside him, occasionally speaking as if aware she must make polite conversation but finding it hard to do so.

At the castle gates, he stopped. "You must make your own way from here, Miss Burney. Can you do it?"

"Yes, yes, indeed. I thank you, sir, for your courtesy."

Winter Ames gave a puzzled look at her, bowed and departed, looking back once to see that Fanny was indeed slowly making her way into the castle.

Fanny moved like a bemused snail through the castle corridors. The King was quiet, no roaring noise, no shouts, no wild pursuit of the robed figure.

Why did he seem to move through her mind as if she had seen him, been near him? She shook her head to push the phantom figure away from her.

Mindy stood up as she came in. "Well, there you are. You've been a time of it. I thought the King had got you."

Fanny shook her head. "I will go to bed, I think. I find myself tired."

"Would you like a hot drink, Miss Burney?"

"No, thank you. I believe I will just go to bed. It was good of you wait up for me."

"My job, miss. And did you get anything about the King from Dr Seaton? Any result from what we sent him?" Charlotte herself put little faith in what she called mumbo-jumbo.

"No. Not yet, Mindy. We must wait."

She submitted herself to Mindy's undressing of her, wondering as she did so why her bodice was buttoned awry, and why she was so conscious of her breasts, although lower down, her skirts and petticoats were neat enough.

Mindy's troubled face, if she could have read it, would have told her.

"Oh god," Mindy was thinking, "she's been rumbled."

And what exactly Miss Minden meant by this pronouncement, she preferred not to dwell upon.

SEVEN

While the two young women slept yet another female creature, even younger than they were, lay dying. Blood was seeping out of her, staining her clothes and the surrounding cobbles. She was unconscious, her last memory was of meeting a friend, or at least someone she knew and trusted, then laughing.

Perhaps to have laughter as your last memory is not so bad.

It was very dark in Tumble Alley off Lovage Lane where she lay so she would be hard to see at night. At the bottom of the alley was a recessed doorway to a large empty room used for storage by the inn in Lovage Lane. The door was locked and rarely opened. It is to be supposed that the killer knew this when he took his victim there before using the knife.

The girl, she was hardly more because she seemed to have the boniness and awkwardness of youth still on her, was wearing a low cut bodice and a thick silk skirt, over all was a loose wrap of wool. Nothing was new or made for her, all the clothes had been through many owners who had, to a certain degree, left their imprint upon them. Thus with the bodice whose first owner must have been a large woman. Now worn by a second or third or fourth lady the folds had to be anchored to-

119

gether with a brooch to preserve any decency. The skirt had been taken up, let down, taken up again so that the hem line dipped and rose like a wave of the sea. The original colour had been blue and was now a sad grey. The cloak of linsey wool was probably the young woman's only contribution to her attire.

Her hair had been tidily dressed when she was still alive, now it was stiff with her own blood. You could tell from her hands that she had done hard, manual work, but she had kept her hands as tidy and neat as she could.

She was called Mary Foster and she worked in the kitchens at the castle in a casual way, when extra was needed. At other times, she took what she could get; sometimes cleaning in the theatre, sometimes helping at the Home for Incurables on the Slough Road. This latter was not a nice establishment because it was where families put the mentally ill or the crippled and helpless whom they could no longer, or did not wish to, look after at home. They were treated as well as possible at the Home for Incurables but it was a rough and ready place with Dr Seaton the only medical man who called to see if he could help.

Mary lodged in a communal lodging house in Abbey Street where she cleaned the house instead of paying rent.

All these details were to be read in *The Windsor Herald* the next day in the report of the discovery of the body. At that point the identity of the victim was not widely known. The few people who had taken notice of her at all grieved for her, but said they had always known she would get into trouble, because she talked to anyone and went out night on her own.

There was no uncertainty about the manner of her death, however; she had been stabbed in the throat and chest, severing an artery.

EIGHT

Charlotte Minden stayed close to Fanny that night, sleeping on the floor. She had slept in worse places. As Fanny slept, she was restless, talking in her sleep, but Mindy could not make out what she was saying.

"Doesn't know herself, I daresay."

Mindy felt she needed advice, she would like to have talked to Sergeant Denny, a man with his feet on the ground. She was wary of the Major, although respecting him. Not a lover of women, she felt, except in his bed. There, she had no doubt, he gave a good account of himself.

She did sleep but was awake as the first light came into the sky. She went across the room to look at Fanny, still asleep.

"I don't know what happened to you last night, my lady, I may have jumped to the wrong idea last night, but drunk I believe you were. Hard to believe of you, who hardly takes a glass of wine and water," she looked affectionately at Fanny's face. "As to what else went on, I hope I was wrong, my dear mistress," she adjusted the quilt which Fanny had thrown off. As she did so, she could see Fanny's throat.

Bruised. Were those teeth marks? No, she imagined too much.

"Upon my word, my mistress, I don't know what went

on last night, nor what you suffered."

She took a step backward to look down at the sleeping face, quiet and remote.

"And how am I ever to ask you? What can I say? Were you rogered last night?" she shook her head. "No, no, I couldn't ask you. And if I did, what could you say to Charlotte Minden your servant."

With a cold, sick feeling at the pit of her stomach, Mindy dressed, checked that her mistress still slept, then stepped out into the corridor.

Before she had the door closed, she heard her mistress calling her back.

Fanny had raised herself on her elbows, pushing her hair from her face.

"Mindy, where are you going?"

"To get fresh water to make you some hot tea."

Fanny said. "I have slept heavily, it feels very late," she touched her forehead. "I think my head aches."

—I hope that is all that ails you, thought Mindy.

"A strange night, Mindy, bad dreams..." She hesitated. "Mindy, I feel as if the King came into them, that perhaps I met him..."

"Lord love us miss, think no more of it at the moment. Lay back," she helped her mistress to lean on the pillows. "And wait till Mindy comes back with your tea."

Once more she went into the corridor.

No one was about. It was still very early and although the scullions would be stirring scarcely anyone else was.

A Windsor mouse ran across her path, not frightening her, there were so many, and so faithful in their attendance on the Court: she had seen one in the Queen's dressing room when she went there once with her mistress. Indeed, it ran over the bundle of clothes that Mindy had carried thither.

She was not now in a mood to notice a mouse.

GWENDOLINE BUTLER

"There is one person I can talk to and that is the Sergeant. No need to put it into hard words, he is a clever man and will understand without being told."

She met no person on the way to Sergeant Denny's room; she rapped on the door.

After a pause, he opened it, in shirt sleeves and carrying his shaving mug and razor.

He looked her in the face, a hard searching gaze. "So? Come in then." He held the door wide. "You are not ill, not too much distressed."

"I am," said Mindy indignantly. "I am indeed."

"Nothing you cannot bear... an old soldier know the rage and ranges of distress. Yours is in the middling range. So, not you, but your mistress."

—I knew he was clever, Mindy thought, told myself so. I am anxious about Miss Burney but it is not so painful as if it was myself.

Also this man is very manly. More so, I believe, than Winter Ames. Different.

Then she reproached herself. It Mindy had a religion, which on the whole, she had not, it was a fierce, strong feeling that there was good and evil in the world, virtue and guilt, and that a many-eyed God was always on the look-out to see the sinner and punish that one. Woman. On the whole it was a woman. Women seemed to find it easier to sin than men.

I am a sinner, she told herself, or I am prepared to be. A sinner with Winter Ames and then with Sergeant Denny.

Denny knows it too.

"Come on then, Miss, what is it?"

"My mistress went out last night, she had the specimens for Dr Seaton," she hesitated. "As you know, for you sent her." Denny bowed his head in acceptance of his responsibility. "So the doctor could say what caused the King's madness. Or claims he will be able... She did not come back. Not for a long long time, Mr Ames."

"The actor?"

"The actor, he went to see if he could find her, he found her walking up the hill." Mindy paused. "She was not herself."

"You had better tell me a bit more," said Denny gravely. "What about the other actor?"

"I don't know anything about him. It was Mr Winter Ames that helped me with my mistress. He's a good gentleman."

"I daresay. A bit more information, please."

Charlotte Minden took a deep breath, she knew that she must be careful what she said to the sergeant, whom she liked and trusted as much as she trusted any man. But a man was a man.

"Not herself?" prompted Denny.

Mindy burst into speech. Get it over with. "My mistress went to see the Doctor as I said, and there," for a second she hesitated. "...and while there she was taken unwell. When she came to herself she found herself walking up Castle Hill not knowing what had gone on..."

"Continue."

"Her clothes were..." again Mindy hesitated. "...not as she had put them on. A little disarranged. She drank a glass of wine with the doctor, so she says."

"Perhaps there is not need to say more," said Denny soberly.

"He is a strange man, the doctor... I think there may have been something in the wine that did not agree with my mistress. She will remember more as she comes to herself, I make no doubt."

"What did Mr Winter Ames have to say?"

"Nothing much. I was too anxious to get my mistress back to her rooms. And I could see he was anxious too."

For a moment neither spoke. When the silence was broken, it was the soldier who spoke. In Mindy's eyes he saw the accusation: whatever happened to Miss Burney is your fault. With thought he put forward his excuse:

"There is a killer loose in this town."

Another pause, then it was Mindy who said: "My mistress said she had a memory... a dream memory, she called it... that the King was there at Dr Seaton's." Her voice sank lower and lower as she spoke.

Even deep in the heart of the castle, far from the royal rooms, it took a brave spirit to accuse the Hanoverian master of the castle, the King himself of being a murderer.

English Kings had been murderers, you could think of Henry VIII as one, but it was unwise to put it into speech. Dangerous, even.

Sergeant Denny was aware that walls have ears in royal courts. The castle was a great place for gossip and rumours which passed around with speed. "Hung, drawn and quartered," he said to himself. "Well, hung or put in the stocks."

There were things you could say, to the right person, about the monarch: that he was mad, that he was too fat, that he liked young women, just as you could say that the Queen was too fat, too German and had had too many children.

But to call the sovereign a sexual maniac was risky.

Even if he was.

More so, if he was.

"It should be possible to discover the King's whereabouts last night," he said cautiously. "It is not easy for the King to get out of the castle unnoticed."

"But he could do it."

Denny was silent. He was a royal servant, after all, the King paid his wages. Or some of it, Mr Pitt added his bit. He was not handsomely paid but he lived well in the castle and enjoyed his work. He had also to remember that there was the Major, a man with a strong voice in what their work was and how they should do it.

"I will speak to Major Mearns."

Mindy knew a promise of action when she heard it and was tactful enough not to press the matter. "Thank you. I must get back to my mistress."

She paused and then looked at him.

"You will know what I know, and when I know it," said Denny. Without a word, Mindy smiled and left him.

Denny said to himself. "Hang the Major. I will speak to Mr Silverline."

Mr Silverline was a body servant to the King, but he was more than that because he was a secretary also, in that he read to the King and wrote his more personal and private letters. True, he was only one of the many about the King, but he was as likely as any to know where the sovereign got to, and why.

He was also a sociable fellow who liked to share a drink, a smoke and a gossip with Major Mearns and Sergeant Denny when he was free. Working hours at the court were long and variable, depending on the royal mood, but equally it was possible to escape.

First Denny consulted the Major. One ignored the Major at one's peril. Beneath the surface ease and jollity, was an iron hard man.

He agreed. "Yes, Silverline will know the King's movements." Taking a turn about the room, he announced that they must get to the bottom of this business. "Find the killer, find out, if we can, and it is not all dream stuff, what happened to Miss Burney."

"A good woman," said Denny. "And a clever one."

"But a lady. Ladies are of no use out in the great world, ladies need looking after."

He walked back from the window. "We must rally, we must rally, there is revolution in the air, the contagion must not spread to here."

"No," agreed Denny.

Mearns stopped dead and gave Denny a long look. "And if it does, we must decide what we shall do. Which side we shall be on. But not much doubt about that."

"And which side would that be?"

"The side which wins," said the Major. "I always fight to win. And so do you, Denny." He laughed, jolly and cynical. He rubbed his hands. "Get some Madeira, get some gin and get Mr Silverline."

Tom Silverline was not hard to entrap. Denny found him in the long gallery, carrying a silken robe into the King's dressing room.

"I'm in a hurry, dear boy, so say what you must. A drink with you and the Major?" He was grey haired, middle-aged man, older than he looked and grown smooth in royal service. As he spoke he stroked the rich silk of the gown with pleasure.

He was amenable to calling in for a drink when off duty, and over a drink of his favoured Madeira wine, he listened to the questions, carefully put, with a quiet, knowing air.

"His Majesty went to his chamber and then his bed early yesterday evening," he said. "Excellent wine this, Major, my dear. But why do you ask?"

"Part of my business, to know about his Majesty's movements," said the Major, smooth in his turn. "Some more wine?"

Tom Silverline did not believe this for a second, and no one knew the gossip and rumours of the castle more than he did.

"Impossible for him to get out unseen?"

"Impossible. A footman sleeps outside his door. And there is the Queen, her bedroom is across the way, very good hearing, she has, Major." He looked at the two men and smiled. "Of course, there is a way for his Majesty if he chose to use it. Kings always have their private ways."

127

"Do they now, Tom." The decanter came forward once more.

"Very private this is." Tom Silverline held on to the moment, enjoying his control. He enjoyed feeling he knew something which the Major did not. "I know my way about the castle, I ought to. I was seven when I came as the humblest of mortals."

"How you have progressed." The Major gave a slight bow.

"There is a hanging on the wall by the bed which hides a door. This is the door to the royal privy. And in the wall of that little room is another door, which leads to a staircase down, down, down, down, to the lower castle ward with a drain… To empty the slops, you see."

"An exit for the royal chamber pot," said Denny, who was a little drunk.

"I used to empty it myself when I was a raw little page," said Tom. "One of my many jobs and I was but a little lad. One sweats, you know, in the royal service." He rolled his eyes. "But nothing to what those who have to hunt with the King can suffer. You should hear what Lord Frederick has to say: the riding and the trotting and the leaping, in the rain, in the ditches, from eight in the morning till after five at night, dripping wet, and offered nothing more than a little barley water at the end of the day."

"*You* know how to get more than a little barley water," observed the Major slyly.

"That I do." His glass was again refilled.

"So you think that if the King wished to take a late night walk, then he could do so."

Tom Silverline took a sip of wine. "The King grew up in the castle, he was a boy here, judge for yourself."

So I will, thought the Major, so I do. But aloud he said nothing.

When Mr Silverline had tottered away, having enjoyed

the best part of two bottles of wine, the Major and Sergeant Denny looked at each other.

"So? What do we think about all this business with Miss
Burney and Doctor Seaton? A fantasy of the female sex?
You spoke to Charlotte Minden, what do you judge?"

Denny thought about it. "Mindy is hard headed young
woman who has seen something, perhaps too much, of
the world, and she was troubled. Something bad did happen."

He continued to think about while he penned a report
to Mr Pitt about life in the Castle.

Being on good terms with the kitchens and knowing that,
although life was hard at court, yet the vittles were generous. They were talking over a late night supper of cold
beef, beer and bread spread thick with good beef dripping.
A dish of pickles was on the table.

"The King is mad, we know, and when mad is eager to
rush towards a female and cuddle her. He talks bawdy.
But does he do more? Is he capable of it?" Major Mearns
was being judicious.

"And if he is, then can we accuse him of raping Miss
Burney and killing sundry other females?"

"Hard to believe," said the Major. "On his own?"

"Aided and abetted by Dr Seaton," said Denny over a
mouthful of beef. "Now there is another strange man. Not
mad but not sane either. In my judgement. Nor Miss
Burney's either, I would say. We sent her to Seaton, you
know. Our fault."

Major Mearns was all for going slow on this.

"But perhaps we should wait till we have seen Miss
Burney."

"She won't speak with us about it," said Denny with conviction.

"But she will speak to Charlotte Minden, who in any case,
will use her own judgement. Tomorrow, Denny, tomorrow."

They were both guilty of sending Fanny into danger, and both men knew it. Silently they accepted that their trade was both ruthless and dangerous.

But when tomorrow came, it was the day the great distemper, the new sickness, came to Windsor.

Oddly, Fanny who had gone to bed in flummoxed and in misery, full of half dreams, awoke calm and cheerful. Had it been Dr Seaton's voice she had heard last night or had she heard the King shouting and hammering on the door?

Charlotte Minden coming to help her dress found her already garbed and asking for some tea and toast.

"For it will be a long day with the Queen, and I must be ready."

"Yes, miss," Charlotte refused to show surprise, although she felt it. "And what about His Majesty, will he be there today?"

Fanny looked as if, for the second, she had forgotten the existence of the King, in her dreams and out of them.

"I will not pretend that I do not know what you mean, Mindy. I have had much to think about: you must remember that I am a novelist. My mind, my imagination, works all the time, dreaming up stories and plots. I was thinking of the poor King, so ill as he is, and he crept into my dreams…"

"Was it a dream then, miss?"

Fanny adjusted her collar. "I had a touch too much wine. I am ashamed, I confess it. I should have taken none. In consequence, I was not myself."

"That you were not, miss."

"Now don't be censorious, Mindy," said Fanny coaxingly. "We all transgress."

Mindy said to herself that to her way of thinking it was not Miss Fanny who had transgressed but others about her. "She won't let herself admit what happened," she told herself. "Can't do it. I have had bad times myself." For

Mindy's life had known hazards, dangers, some provoked, but most undeserved. As Fanny's was. "I blame myself. And the Sergeant, for letting Fanny take the sample of the King's blood to Dr Seaton. It was ill advised, wrong, and has brought its punishment with it."

A tap on the door announced the arrival of tea and toast. Mindy took it from the manservant. She poured the tea into the cup, one of Miss Burney's own china set, creamy white with delicate flowers. Her own mouth was dry and thirsted for a cup, but she must wait.

Fanny took the cup, her head ached but she meant to say nothing about it. "Sometimes," she said in a low voice, "one loses the sense of one's own identity."

"I have laundered your shift, Miss Burney, and repaired the torn tape," Mindy said in a tough, unaccepting voice: what was done, however done, had to be accepted as having happened. She would have nothing of dreams and imaginings.

Fanny gave her a quick aware glance: torn shifts were real, not born of her novelist's fancy. She dropped her head while sipped the hot tea.

"Don't expect much service today, miss, there is sickness going around the kitchens. Sore throats, dizziness, spots." Mindy continued her saga while handing over her mistress's breakfast which privately she thought hardly food enough for a bird. Her own more substantial repast had already been consumed below stairs: a slice of cold beef, a cut of ham and several thick slices of bread. Warmed small beer was always there to drink, but Mindy did not take it. She drank tea when she could get it and hot chocolate, but these, being costly drinks, were not always available to those who worked in the castle. True there was a private supply for the Princesses and the Queen which was pillaged more often than they knew. When she had finished simultaneously sustaining and alarming her mistress

131

she would go back to sup a hot cup herself.

"It is not healthy down there in the kitchens and the pantries, I have always thought it a poor place to work... heated with the ovens and the spits over the open fires and damp underfoot at the same time."

"It's the river Thames," said Fanny absently. "We are so near the river."

"It is not the river." Mindy was brisk. "It is the drains. That is where the sickness comes from. The rest of the town is healthy, you will see."

But she was wrong: the sickness, the new ailment, was everywhere, rampant, already on the move from house to house and street to street. Even as Mindy went down into the kitchen to sit drinking some tea, a child in yet another house was falling sick, and then another was showing signs and then another. Not all the victims were children, for while she stirred the pot for another cup, the married couple in another house down the street were sickening. The new disease had legs, had wings it moved so fast.

Later, when Dr Seaton was being questioned by the Major and Denny, he said: "This illness has been sitting in the population for some time before springing out. They take some time to show these infections and then it is everywhere." And he nodded his head sagely.

The Major and Sergeant Denny had noticed this for themselves as they strode through the town. Twice, thrice, a wagon carrying a coffin passed them. Empty coffins as yet, but ready for use.

"They are on with the business early today," said the Major.

The two men had come down the hill to Dr Seaton's house that morning to talk to him. Denny felt some awkwardness at asking a man if he had ravished a young lady and even greater reluctance to ask it the King himself had been there too.

The Major however felt no such compunction and embarked on his questioning without delay. True, he wrapped things up with a little flattery.

"Remember," he had said to Sergeant Denny as they stood on the doorstep: "We sent Miss Fanny down with the King's piss pot so we must be open about it; no doubt he guesses our part. So we make him talk with authority to which we bow, then we lead him into the other matter."

Dr Seaton was tidily, even elegantly dressed, in fine broadcloth, his hair tied back with black now, neat slippers with a silver buckles on his feet, and the scent of pomade hanging about him.

His face was close shaven but there were deep shadows under his eyes. He was not as happy as he was trying to appear—a touch of conscience, Denny thought, we shall have him now, a man with conscience will want it purged in the end.

Fanny would have said at once that last night he had been full of wine and today was sober.

"Major Mearns, at your service, sir."

Dr Seaton was also busy, Denny observed. They had been shown into a small room lined with books, a room Fanny would remember when her working memory came back. On the walls were several drawing and pictures which Denny studied. On the table stood a large black bag filled with bottles and jars and gleaming instruments. There was one hooked piece with a black handle which made Denny's eyes water, wondering what part of the anatomy it was made to enter and what to hook out. The doctor had learnt his medicine in Edinburgh and Geneva, he had heard, in which cities there was much learning. And Seaton, after all, was a Scottish name.

Scottish doctors were well thought of. Windsor has apothecaries, midwives, surgeons who are akin to barbers, and the King's doctor who comes from London, but otherwise, Dr Seaton is the doctor for the gentry. As Major Mearns once remarked: he kills the best people.

"I know you, Major. You live in the Castle."

Mearns nodded. "I work there."

"The King has many servants."

The Major did not think of himself as a servant, still less did Denny, but neither said anything. They were at their most alarming when secretly swallowing insults.

"Miss Burney came down from the Castle last night to visit you, doctor."

Dr Seaton did not answer.

"It was at our request, Dr Seaton."

Hammer away at his name, he told himself, they don't like that, those with a conscience and something on it. He had discovered this in India where the darker the skin the more a man shrank from having his name repeated. Even those with nothing on their conscience. Of which there were mighty few, for most men can be convinced that they are guilty of something.

"At your request, I believe." He would swear that the doctor flinched. "We obtained specimens from His Majesty."

Dr Seaton nodded his head.

"And did you discover anything from them?"

"It takes time to establish a result... but I can tell you that the King, bless his majesty, is gravely ill."

So we supposed, thought Denny, but is he mad and a likely killer of young women?

"And would this illness cause the wildness from which we know he suffers?" The Major had chosen his words carefully; Wildness sounds so innocuous, not speaking loudly of rape and murder.

"I find this difficult to say." He did not turn to look at them but occupied himself with busily packing yet more bottles into his big black bag.

"Come now, doctor, everyone knows the King is mad,"

said Mearns, losing his temper. "What we want to know is: is he dangerously mad?"

And ask yourself why we are putting this question to you, said Sergeant Denny to himself. From the colour receding in Dr Seaton's face, he deduced that the doctor was indeed asking himself this.

"I have heard that he pursues ladies," he said cautiously. "I am not sure that could be called madness. It depends on the degree."

Denny said coarsely: "But you have never seen him at it?"

"Certainly I have not."

The denial direct, the lie direct, the Sergeant thought as he looked at Major Mearns who gave a shrug which said Who knows?

"Miss Burney," he began, then stopped at a warning look from the Major.

Dr Seaton concentrated on his medical bag, just raising his head to tell them that when he had finished work on the specimens brought down by Miss Burney he would tell them what conclusions he had come to. As for Miss Burney, that clever lady novelist whom he admired, he trusted she had got back to the castle safely? "I would gladly have sent my servant home with her but Mrs Bartlett has been one of the first victims of this new sickness, and was already unwell."

Mrs Bartlett, indeed, thought the Sergeant, who knew the lady by sight, that wizened old creature, who is reputed to go out with the doctor as nurse when he attends some doubtful confinements with ladies who wish for no publicity. For Sergeant Denny knew more about Mrs Bartlett and some of the good doctor's activities than he had told Major Mearns. Not every baby conceived came to term, nor every child delivered survived the trauma.

But no doubt the Major knew more too than he had said.

135

They were colleagues but kept their own secret stores of information. No one who had fought in India and learnt its ways could be other than secretive. India taught you self-preservation which often meant knowing just that much more than your neighbour.

Dr Seaton picked up his bag and motioned them to the door. "I must be away on my calls... I shall be very busy. This is a bad time, you must understand that the sickness will spread and spread. Contagion will reach everywhere. The sickness will reach out and touch every family with its hot fingers." As he spoke, Dr Seaton's old manservant tottered in to hand the doctor his top coat and tall hat. The doctor held out his arms and slowly inserted himself inside the coat, then he took his hat in his hand.

It had to be admitted, the Sergeant thought, that Dr Seaton did not look so distressed as might have been expected. Excited, was more like it.

"What about you, Dr Seaton," said Major Mearns, as if he had had the same thought, "going about to the worst afflicted households as you do, will you not be in danger?"

"Every man will be in danger," said the doctor solemnly, "but I have taken my precautions."

Catching his breath, Denny decided that one of the precaution was a good long sup of brandy.

The doctor was used to death, of course. He had a skeletal hand on his desk to weigh down his letter and a child's small skull rested on the shelf above.

"Perhaps the King should leave Windsor," said Major Mearns. "But you say he is a sick man?"

"Indeed he is, although I have not got the exact nature of his illness yet. However, I should advise the Court to go to Kew, but that the infection will certainly go with him."

"You seem certain of a great deal," said Denny.

"I have made a special study of plagues and of this scarlet fever in particular."

136

"That's the name of it, is it?"

"It is its colour." The handkerchief with which he mopped his brow was of fine cambric. Money no object, thought the cynical Denny.

"And shall we all die scarlet, then? Those that do die, that is. I take it there is a good deal of death?"

"Upon my word, you make sport with a serious matter." The doctor was walking towards the door, motioning his visitors before him. "But you shall find out."

They were being ushered out when he said: "About Miss Burney, she did get back to the Castle safely?"

The Major weighed his words. "Her maid, Charlotte Minden, tells me she was more than a little…" he paused with deliberation, "more than a little disturbed. Or did she say disarranged? Or both?"

"I must hope she is not a victim of this new disease," said the doctor with cold courtesy. "She must be watched." His manservant came up to him with a hand held out, muttering of Lady Derbyshire and Sir Harry Hope, "Excuse me now, I have several sick to see, and here comes old Joseph with a list of others. Sir Harry, eh, dear me, dear me."

"What did we get from that?" asked Sergeant Denny as they walked away. Dr Seaton going off in his carriage to tend his patients. "From the sound of it, he didn't think much of Sir Harry's chances."

"Nor of much else, the lying old toad. He could be the killer we are looking for himself, and I would like him to be, for I declare I dislike him intensely."

"Sick, sick, sick."

"He knows more about the King than he admits, and more about Miss Burney too. But does he know more about the murder of the two women?"

"Did you notice that on the wall of that room there was

a drawing of a young woman? Not from the life, I judge, a fanciful portrait of the new French school." Denny liked pictures of women himself.

"No, never looked."

"You should have done, sir, she had a likeness to Miss Burney." Since the Sergeant was not much given to imaginings, the Major took him seriously.

"The doctor did say he admired her," said the Major thoughtfully.

"So he did. How much seems to hang around Miss Burney."

The two men walked back to the Castle in silence. As the silhouette of the great tower loomed up in front of them, the Major broke the silence: "We must speak to Miss Burney."

Fanny and Mindy took a nuncheon together after Fanny had dressed the Queen. "Not that I do dress," she said. "My part is more humble, only a peeress or the daughter of a duke may dress her Majesty, I merely receive the clothes from the wardrobe woman and hand them over to Lady Susan Waldegrave. Oh my poor mistress, never can I forget her countenance, pale, ghastly pale she looked, her whole frame disordered."

"You were not well yourself, miss."

"I had passed endless hours in conjectures too horrible to admit."

Ah, so you do admit it, thought Mindy, that's a step forward.

"When the page said I must come to the Queen I could hardly get myself along, I felt dizzy, almost to falling. But I became more collected."

It had to be admitted that Miss Burney now looked quite herself, cheeks pink, hair neatly arranged, dress *pointe devisee*.

Mindy felt a pang of reluctant admiration. Reluctant only because she still did not know what had gone on last night.

"The Queen is ill…" Fanny lowered her voice. "I think she is afraid of the King."

Mindy let her go on, saying nothing else except with her large, blue, expressive eyes. But her dear Miss Fanny was not one able to read the more cynical, worldly expression in her maidservant's eyes.

"She thinks he might kill her."

Mindy achieved a look of surprise, although she did not feel it. She had begun to realise that violence and sudden death hung about Courts and was not an invention of Shakespeare, several of whose plays she had seen London actors perform.

"She knows that some English Kings have killed their wives. She knows that her husband's great grandfather wanted his wife dead."

German, thought the cynical Mindy, not one of us. In the rough, insular world along the Thames where she had grown up, they had little respect for Kings and Queens. Germans all, for the riverside Londoners there had not been an English Queen since Queen Anne and she was dead. If it had come to a revolution they would not have been for cutting off his head, just send him back to Hanover whence he came in the first place, and let him quarrel with the King of Prussia. You could always get another King. If you wanted one.

"Perhaps the Queen is sickening with the new illness," Mindy suggested, while keeping her thoughts to herself.

"No," Fanny shook her head. "She has no fever, but I think Lady Susan may be; she was raging hot and trembling."

Their nuncheon was a cosy affair, a tray on the table with cold meat, cake and fruit with coffee to drink. Fanny sat at the table and Mindy hovered but quietly eating as much as her mistress. Both pretended this informality between mistress and maid was not happening. Life at court, where Fanny found herself a humble servant to the Queen, was ironing out the distinction between mistress and maid.

Outside the disease was showing itself here and there while laying the seeds of future eruptions with speed. Sex, rank and income, the infection showed no discrimination. The errand boy with the basket sickened as did Sir Thomas Heavistone, the baronet and banker newly settled in a grand new house overlooking the Thames. Nurse Jerrold, monthly nurse to the ladies of the gentry, was beginning to feel ill.

The malady even touched the Theatre Royal where Winter Ames found his colleague James Manston irritable. Twitchy, was how Ames put it to himself. "We shall have a poor house indeed," was all Manston said, his voice irritable. "If this sickness goes about longer." He put his hand to his head. "I am not feeling too uppish myself. I shall have to see old Seaton. He's best doctor around here."

But Winter Ames, who was thinking with anxiety of both Miss Burney and her maid Charlotte Minden, had not much answer to give, except to hope that, if taken ill, they did not call in Dr Seaton.

Mindy was at the door, the tray in her hands ready to carry to the kitchens below, when there was a rap on the door.

She looked at her mistress.

"Open it, Mindy."

Major Mearns and Sergeant Denny stood outside, in their customary stance, with Denny one pace behind the Major. There was no hint in subservience here, though.

"Miss Burney, may we talk with you."

Mindy held the door open wide as the two came in. Behind her, Fanny had risen to her feet.

"Better to be open," began the Major, who only was so

when it suited him, no man could keep a secret longer. "The King is mad, could be dangerously so, confirms Dr Seaton… a strange fellow himself by the by but a good doctor and scientist, they all say so… And dangerous his Majesty could be, don't say he is, but has the means, to be loose at night." He gave a little laugh. "Treason, I talk here, but among friends. A good thing walls do not have ears." Another laugh. "Or I should be hung, drawn and quartered. If they still do that, do they, Denny?"

"I daresay," said Denny phlegmatically. "If they fancy to."

"I am glad to see you looking so well, Miss Burney."

Mindy spoke quickly. "She is ever so much better, quite herself." And indeed there was a calm and a solidity and a quietness about Fanny that made Mindy think she had been mistaken about what had happened to Miss Burney and that she had not been raped.

It was true, she told herself, that growing up in her own rough world she was inclined to think the worst of any situation because the worst it usually was.

And there was a situation here, even if Miss Burney seemed happily to have swept it all away. Something had happened and Mindy would like to know what. Being a lady, seemed to mean you always thought the best and not the worst. Or were too innocent to imagine the worst.

"So I have told you the matter as I see it, with as much information as we could get from Dr Seaton."

"Which was not much," put in Denny. "Things are stewing up. That's my opinion."

Major Mearns asked Miss Burney to let him know when Dr Seaton told her of the results of his work on the poor King's specimen, and he would do the same. Then they would decide whom, if anyone, they should tell.

As he opened the door to depart, there was a sound of loud voices and the thud of hurrying feet.

141

"Get back, miss," he ordered, holding the door.

Up came the King, followed at a distance by his valet and Lord in Waiting.

"Miss Burney, Miss Burney, I have come to you." The King leaned on the door frame, steadying himself with his hand. He was dressed in a dark suit with the Garter draped across. "I am here, my dear miss." He tried to push past the Major. "Let me pass, sir, I am your Sovereign."

Lord Somerton and the manservant came up at that point. "Sire, let me take you away."

"Go away, Somerton," said the King irritably.

The King, who was hot from running, dragged a white handkerchief from his pocket to mop his brow.

It had been white cambric once, but now was blotched with blood in a great stain.

"Miss Burney," he began again, but his voice was weaker; Somerton and the manservant had their arms around and were gently drawing him away. Down the corridor came another couple of men.

"Say nothing of this, Mearns," commanded Lord Somerton, over his shoulder. "Good day to you, Miss Burney."

"Did you see the blood?" asked Denny as they walked away. In the distance, they heard the King roaring away and now the words were more obscene.

Mearns nodded. "Dried blood… some hours old, if I am a judge."

As he was, he had seen plenty in the wars.

In the streets outside the red disease was spreading, gaining recruits with every hour. The errand boy was lying on a truckle bed, alternately shivering and sweating. In the theatre, one of the cast was aching and terrified but determined to perform, in the Court itself one of the Queen's dressers was showing irrefutable symptoms of the disease. Dr Seaton hurried from sickbed to sickbed, treating the poor who could not pay with as much care as his richer patients. He showed no fear of the infection for himself, which was not true of all the medical men in the town, one or two of whom had already decided to travel into the country while Dr Seaton and Mr James, the humble apothecary from Lower Thames street laboured on.

And in Tumble Alley the blood around the dead woman thickened and grew stale, even while the killer grew in confidence, full of imagery.

Magician, King, the all-powerful one.

Hungry for another killing.

NINE

Where there is a dead body, lying in the darkest recesses of an alley, murder has to be suspected, since bodies do not move themselves. Even saints, Sergeant Denny said to himself, have to have the job done for them. And when the body, although dressed as a woman, proves to be a man, and that man a member of the royal household, then you are in trouble.

The sergeant got down on his haunches to study the body again. Was he glad he had found it... him or her?

He was in a sombre mood since he and the Major had that morning received a message from the Constable that another dead woman, the third had been found in an alley off Lovage Lane.

Now here was another body, this time in Tumble Alley.

It was certainly interesting. His attention had been drawn to it by a small boy who, out delivering a parcel, had gone down the alley to piss, but had rushed out screaming.

Denny, having stepped out for some air, away from the pipe of the Major's which puffed away forever, had caught the lad in mid scream.

His thoughts had been running over the events of yesterday. The mysteries of India, which he had noted and

145

enjoyed, had nothing to compare with the mysteries of Windsor, he had reckoned. The mad, shouting, running King, the dubious Dr Seaton, the murders, the disease now springing into almost every house, a complex of puzzles not yet making a pattern he could comprehend. There usually was a pattern in life if you could recognise it.

He caught sight of a bit of the pattern now.

He knew the face and had to admit to surprise. The last man he would have suspected of fancying a change of sex.

The coroner would have to sit on this one, and then it would all come out. Or would it? Things could be kept quiet and the Castle would certainly want this handled discreetly.

But the sergeant found a radical voice inside him which said the townspeople, the ordinary citizens had a right to know.

There was an interesting question here; had the victim been killed because he was thought to be a woman, or had he died because he was a man dressed as a woman? One way or another he had certainly paid for his pleasures.

As a man, he had dressed well, as a woman you had to say he was bedraggled.

Sergeant Denny debated what he should do: no doubt, he should go to Sir George, the magistrate, or call on the Constable of the Watch who kept the King's Peace in Windsor and arrested any criminals he could catch.

Certainly these gentleman should be told, but he thought he would go to the Major first. Major Mearns was clever, as was Denny himself, and neither man had a high opinion of the other two gentlemen of law.

The errand boy was no longer wailing, but was staring at the corpse and then at Denny.

"It's all right, lad," Denny said. "You did right to call out. What's your name?"

"Will Tarden, sir."

"And where do you live?"

Denny sat back on his heels and surveyed the corpse.

"With Mr Tandy, the tailor, sir. In Jewry Court. And my mother sells fish in the market." The smell of fish hung about him and his little barrow.

"I know Mr Tandy."

"He's a good master, sir."

"I know it." And Mr Tandy knew Sergeant Denny. "Get back to him, tell what you found, ask him to send to the constable and tell him that Sergeant Denny is dealing with it. Then don't talk about it."

"No, sir."

"And come back here. I may have need of you. You can leave your barrow."

Of course, the lad would talk, not to be expected otherwise, but by that time, action would have been taken.

Meanwhile, Denny sat back on his heels and looked at the body. He had not come out to the town just get fresh air. He had another intention.

The Major and Sergeant Denny worked together in a friendly fashion, knew their own working history as soldiers but did not exchange confidences. True, Denny knew that the Major's young wife had died in childbirth, and Mearns knew that Denny had been jilted. What he did not know was that one reason Denny was glad to work in Windsor was that his grandmother lived there. Not far away in a neat little cottage in the Great Park.

He had intended to walk there and pay her a visit. Partly as duty and a pleasure, she liked to see him, as he liked to see her, but also because she was a remarkably well informed old woman. She had brought him up, been as a mother to him. For all he knew, she might be his mother, since he had never known any other. But she said his mother had died when he was a baby and since she was a truthful woman, he believed her. You're a good lady, ma, he said to himself. He had said it last time they had met and she had said: "You ought to find yourself a nice young gal and forget the past."

I have got my eye on one now, ma, he said to himself. You wait. A handsome young woman and clever and knows her own mind. One Charlotte Minden.

He sat there, looking at the dead body and thinking of a woman of spirit. "I'm a romantic, that's the trouble with me." He stood up; he could see a trio of men advancing down the alley.

He knew them for a magistrate, and two constables. He knew this particular magistrate, Mr Butters, and he knew one of the constables, James Drew, the other was unknown.

"Mr Butters," he offered the magistrate something between a bow and a nod. Where was Sir George, the senior magistrate? But why ask, fled to his country estate to avoid the infection. Not for him was a corpse in Tumble Alley.

"Well, Sergeant Denny, what have you here for us?" The magistrate drew close to the body but did not kneel down to look, motioning to James Drew to do the job.

"Jem," Denny said to the constable. "Got a surprise for you here. Tom not with today?"

"Tom was took bad," he looked over his shoulder. "This is Mr Paskett who has come over from Eton to help out."

So the infection is spread to the law and will soon spread further, if I am not mistaken. Mr Butters does not look well.

148

"And who have we got here?" Drew was brisk and business like. "A woman of the town by the look of her."

"You have a surprise coming," said Denny.

The constable's hands were moving over the body, Denny saw him frowning. He pulled at the bodice, touched the hair, and then sat back. "So that's the way of it."

"You know him?"

"Him?" said Mr Butters.

They ignored him, a fate that often came the way of this particular magistrate.

"Take a look, Paskett. Seen one like this before?"

Paskett stepped forward, gazed and then delivered a judgement. "Not dead, no." He moved back. "Otherwise, yes. You get everything in Eton High Street, but he'd be better dressed with us."

"Ah there is a pleasure in the gutter," said Denny. "And you know that as well as I do."

"So that's how it was with Lord Frederic?" Paskett shook his head. "I knew him as a boy in Eton. A bit wild then, the old Marquess was worried about him. Wild, wild."

Mr Butters fussed up. "We must move the body. Lord Frederic, oh my goodness. Get a litter, James Drew."

"One is coming."

"And where will he go?"

"There is a room behind the police house in Market Street. Bodies go there, sir, until the coroner has sat upon them."

Mr Butters knew this as well as anyone, but Lord Frederic was an aristocrat. A bloody, murdered dead one, to be true, and dressed up in ragged clothes as a woman, but still the son of a Marquis.

"He ought to lie in the Castle." Mr Butters wrung his hands.

"What do you think?" James looked at Sergeant Denny.

"I think not," said Denny. "He's for you."

"We are rather rich in bodies at the moment," said James Drew.

The two men looked at each other: this was the fourth body, killed in the same way.

"I think we can make room for him," he said grimly.

They watched as the litter, covered in a cloth, was carried away.

"His lordship must be identified," cried Mr Butters. "Some member of the family or of the Royal Household must do it." He had a flash of pleasurable thought that he might, by this means, be brought in contact with someone Royal.

"I will speak to Major Mearns," suggested Denny.

"Oh yes," nodded Jem. "We all know what will happen then: the Major will have him all tidied up, tucked up in bed, and then quietly interred." He shook his head. "No, not this time. Can't be done."

All of them silently went behind the litter which was loaded on to a cart. By this time, a small crowd had assembled to watch. Among them, eyes wide and alert, was the boy who had found the body.

"I went to Mr Tandy, sir, and he went to the constable."

"I know." Denny put his hand on his shoulder. "What is your name again?"

"Will, sir. Will Tarden."

"Have you done your errands?"

Clearly the lad had not, he was standing by his small handcart on which parcels, smelling of fish, were still sitting. Well, they could sit a bit longer. Denny handed over a coin. "Give a message from me to Major Mearns at the Castle."

"They won't let me in."

"I daresay you know a way in." He handed over another coin.

Will put it in a pocket and nodded, saying nothing.

A discreet lad, thought Denny, with an eye to the main chance. He will go far.

"Yes, well, I will tell you to find the Major and what to say: you may tell him about the body."

"They say it's a lord from the Castle," said the boy eagerly.

"Do they indeed, you tell him that too, then. And say that Sergeant Denny is pursuing an enquiry."

"Done, sir."

"And take your fish with you."

He watched as Will sped away, wielding the barrow like an Ancient Briton driving his chariot into battle. Away behind him, going slowly, the shrouded body of the last victim rumbled over the cobbles. An arm and hand fell free and was roughly shoved back.

"Better to be a dead fish than a dead lord," thought Denny.

In a small clearing in the Great Park, there was a tiny, low cottage. Smoke was blowing from the chimney, a red geranium stood on the window sill, it was flowering profusely.

"Gran's still got her touch with plants," Denny said to himself.

He knocked on the door, pushed it open and marched in. A tiny plump woman in a long black skirt with a shawl around her was stirring something evil smelling in a saucepan.

Around her was a group of mixed size dogs: a low slung basset hound, a wall-eyed white coated terrier, several foxhounds, and a couple of nondescript mongrels. A cat sat by the fire.

"Ma," said Denny. "What are you cooking there?"

She did not raise her head from the pan, but continued to stir. "Food for the dogs."

"They eat well."

Now she did look at him. "No need to be rude, they have to eat what I can get them, the gamekeeper lets me have this and that, and the dogs like it. Want to eat with them?"

He came over and gave her a hug. "First things first, how are you ma?" He studied her face. "Feeling all right? No spots?"

"So that's what you came to see me for? To see if I have spots on my face?" Her brown, healthy, but surprisingly unwrinkled face had no spot on it.

"That first, there is a bad illness on the move, I wouldn't want you to have it, ma."

The dogs were eating from one large dish and the cat had leapt down, seized a piece of meat from beneath the nose of a hound and leapt away with it.

"I haven't, nor I won't. You look to yourself."

"I reckon I had everything in India."

In spite of the wrangling way they talked to each other, there was a great affection between them.

"More dogs than ever, I see, ma."

Mrs Denny spared the hungry mob, who had already cleared their dish, a quick look. "You can't let a hound be shot because he can't hunt any more, can't keep up with the pack on account of a sore leg. Samson here was a fine hound in his day, always first on the scent. I reckon he's got the screws like I have." She did hobble around. "So what did you come for?"

"You will have heard about the killings, the killings of women?"

In spite of the isolation of her home, Mrs Denny heard all the gossip of town and court from the keepers in the

152

park and the royal huntsmen. She was a noted curer of dogs and cats and even the royal spaniels came to her for treatment.

She nodded. "Word has come around."

"And do they say who is the killer?"

She shrugged with one shoulder, her head on that side, a characteristic gesture, one Denny remembered from childhood.

"How can they know?"

"Guess?"

She shook her head. And then: "But what people say is that it started when a young person came from London to the Castle."

Denny frowned. "Do they blame this young person?"

"No, not blame, of course not blame. You can be innocent, unknowing but the cause. The fancy is that this young person is the innocent cause."

"And the name?"

"No name."

No name.

"Someone from London," she said. "It's the same with animals: put a new dog in the pack, and especially if it be a new breed, then there is trouble. Dogs, pigs, sheep, people... all the same."

Denny nodded. It happened in the regiment too. Men were hostile to anyone different. The army was not a place in which to be different. All the same, he did not fancy the idea if it applied to Fanny Burney and to Charlotte Minden.

"Do you know of Lord Frederic Bertie?"

"I've heard talk... in trouble is he?"

"Yes," Denny nodded.

"It's not to be wondered at," she shook her head.

"He's dead, ma, killed."

"Poor soul, poor soul. He wasn't his father's son, you

see. His mother, the Princess Maria, she'd go with anyone, or so they said, I looked after her dogs for her, that's
all I know of my own knowing. The true aristocrat can
do anything, anything and no harm comes to them but
you see Lord Frederic wasn't one, his father was a
groom. He couldn't expect the same luck in life. There's
rules you know, you get it in the kennels and in the
stables, you can't go against them."

And the sergeant, while not liking what he heard, had
to admit that the sins of the aristocracy were not visited so heavily upon them as on lesser men.

His grandmother seemed able to accept all this, but
the sergeant's rough and angry spirit could not.

Poor Lord Frederic, he thought, done for the moment
he was born. Or even before, in that fatal conjunction
of his mother and the groom. What a pity he couldn't
have had a prettier frock to die in.

Denny went back to find Major Mearns who knew about
the death of Lord Frederic. He listened to all that Denny
had to say.

"So that's the way of it, how the town sees it: these
killings started with the arrival of Miss Burney. What a
force she has been."

And all the more powerful for being unconscious of
it, Denny thought.

TEN

Fanny Burney and Charlotte Minden sat together in Fanny's room while Mindy dressed her mistress's hair for the afternoon waiting on the Queen.

The new illness was everywhere, it was raging in Lower Bell Yard and the streets and alleys such as Pie Alley and Ramillies Cut around it, all where Fanny visited with blankets and clothes, it had spread to the Court. The first story that this was a disease of the poorest people was soon dismissed. Lawyers, clerics, doctors themselves were falling ill with the pink spots. The King was said to be sickening, but everyone knew that his illness might be something quite other than a sore throat and deep pink rash. Indeed his voice could still be heard in the distance, ranting on.

It was rumoured that what with one thing and another, the court might remove to Kew.

"But Her Majesty means to put a brave front on, for the moment anyway," said Fanny, sitting in a white sheet so that in a few minutes her hair could be powdered. Both she and Mindy detested this fashion and sneezed and coughed as it was performed. "She has asked for some of the actors to come up from the theatre and perform some trifle. No one wants it to happen but we all must watch."

Fanny had been writing when Mindy came into the room to tell her it was full time to dress. She had a small writing table in the window where the light was good… her eyes were poor, an inheritance from her father, Dr Burney, and

155

candlelight was not good to write by.

But in truth, she had done no writing while at Court. Her duties there seemed to sit on the imagination so heavily that no story could struggle out. Now scenes and sentences were forming in her mind.

A young woman again, ready to be wooed, and yes, a lover there waiting. But they would be parted. In a novel, if not in real life, it was always better for lovers to be parted.

Fanny smiled as she wrote, the words coming easily. She did not notice at first when Mindy came into the room.

Mindy stood for a moment watching Fanny. She could feel the power hanging around that absorbed figure. A mist of it, a miasma, felt if not seen. It spread out from Fanny, almost like warmth.

Mindy had always thought of herself as the strong one, understood that she protected her mistress who was made, as the gentry were, of weaker material. Not so, she knew it now.

"She could ride through a revolution," she said to herself, watching the absorbed, delicate profile. Mindy was not clear where this energy came from or what had released it. Could it be the episode, that strange episode with Dr Seaton which she still did not understand, nor Fanny speak of?

Dr Seaton now, there was a strange man. "I do not trust you, Dr Seaton," she said aloud. "You think yourself too important."

Fanny looked up. "There you are, Mindy. What did you say?"

"Just to remind you it is time to do your hair. After you have dressed."

"The powder, the powder, miss."

"I hate the powdering."

It was one of the tiresome things about Court life that the hair must be powdered. Elsewhere in sophisticated circles, hair was worn free and natural.

Romantic. But the Court was stuck in the century before, formal, strict, and most certainly not romantic.

It was one thing that allowed Mindy to rejoice that she was of the serving class: maid servants did not powder their hair: footmen did or went wigged, but not women.

Fanny allowed herself to be dressed without saying much.

"Are you tired, miss?" Mindy put her head on one side. "Bored?"

"I am writing, I have begun again..." Fanny's voice was light, cheerful yet preoccupied.

"What's it about?"

"My theme? What it always is: Innocence."

Well, thought Mindy, as she went with enthusiasm at the powdering, you might have plenty to say about innocence, but a whole three volumes?

"And Experience," went on Fanny, deep in thought.

Ah, that's more like, thought Mindy, you can do a lot with experience. But three volumes? Can Miss fill three volumes? Even I could hardly do one.

"Clever," said Mindy. "You are clever, Miss Burney."

"No, not clever, good writing is not clever, cleverness spoils it."

Mindy did not understand this, but she was willing to try. She frowned: "Like embroidery of a rich satin dress would spoil the silk?"

"Something like that, Mindy." You are clever yourself, Fanny thought, wondering if she could shape Mindy into a character in her book. Mindy deserved better of life than being a serving maid. She looked at Mindy's bright, concentrated face as she worked and knew that, for a woman, so much depended on love and marriage.

As true for me as for her, she thought. It should not be so, but it is.

"Are you happy with your lot in life, Mindy?" she asked suddenly. "No, not happy, that is too much to ask... Are you content?"

Mindy smiled at her. "Both happy and content, Miss. I had a poor start in my life and that there were bad times in it, I do not deny. But I had the good luck to come into Dr Burney's household and to be given to you as your maid."

"Not given, Mindy," said Fanny gently. "Not given away like a present. A person cannot be given away."

Mindy answered stoutly: "A poor person can be, Miss Burney, a poor child can be apprenticed to a bad master and be tied for years, ill fed and beaten. I might have been sent to that fate."

Fanny was silent, in her sheltered life, if she had considered foundling, child apprentices, she had probably thought how fortunate they were to be put in the way of making an honest living.

"Mindy," she said. "If this great sickness goes on, I mean to go out into the town and help to nurse. I must do this, Mindy."

"What about the Queen?"

"She will hide in Kew Palace."

"If you go, then I will go too," said Mindy gloomily, feeling that she had not fought forward, like a lost cat looking for a good home, to be nursing the sick. Nurses were not an admired group where she came from, as likely to rob and kill their patients as cure them: that was the philosophy of the streets.

"There will be risk of infection."

"I daresay I had the pink spot before I was walking, we mostly did where I come from."

There was a tap, a double tap, quiet but commanding on the door.

Mindy went to open it and there stood Sergeant Denny. In a low voice he asked to speak to her and her mistress.

Mindy drew the door behind her and stepped out into the passage. "Mistress is dressing and can see no one."

"I can talk to you then, Miss Minden. It is right you should know; there has been another murder." He stopped there, not quite sure how much to tell her.

"A woman again?"

He spoke half the truth: "Appeared so."

Charlotte Minden knew a prevarication when she heard one. "Come, Sergeant Denny, I believe you know the difference between a man and a woman."

"He wore a woman's dress," said Denny tersely.

"Oh, one of those. We had plenty of those where I come from."

"Everywhere, I suppose."

"Even in the army," she was probing, Denny recognised this but did not know how to respond.

"One or two, but they fought bravely."

"A cod woman, that's what we called them," she said, half sadly, for she had known and felt affection for one such. "Like a whipping, did he?" she asked knowledgeably, "and it went too far?"

"He was stabbed, a knife was used on him."

"Ah, now that is sad. No pleasure there for him, not even in his last gasp. Some have had a great thrill of pleasure at the last," she said.

"You amaze me, miss."

"Not I." Mindy stared at Denny. "You know this person, recognised him, I can see it in your eyes, hear it in your voice." Her mind was racing. It was likely that she too knew the name of the victim.

"There is a club for such people," she said suddenly.

"How do you know that?"

"Never mind how I know, I do know. It is down by Eton

bridge, on the Eton side of the river. They call it the Toy Club."

Denny knew of the club, of course, it was the sort of knowledge that he and the Major garnered. There were many clubs, some tiny, some rich and large. Some for working men and artisans and others for the gentry and aristocrats. Smoking clubs, drinking clubs, gambling clubs, or a row of chairs in the local drinking house where you met your friends and read the papers. Clubs came in all sorts and sizes; they were the fashion of the day.

And there were clubs like Toys, which the Sergeant knew was more popularly named: Boys for Toys. A nasty place.

Fanny appeared at the door, a cotton gown about her shoulders, her hair half dressed… "What is this? What goes on, Mindy?"

Sergeant Denny broke in: "There has been another murder, Miss Burney. Major Mearns thinks it better if you and Miss Mindy do not go out into the town alone. Better not to go at all."

Fanny drew herself up. "It is not for Major Mearns to tell me so. I shall go," she turned to Mindy. "I heard what you said about clubs, I did not understand what you were saying but it concerns this murder. How do you know these things, Mindy?"

"Servants know everything, Miss Burney. Of course they do."

"And talk to each other?"

Mindy was silent.

"So you were told what you know by a fellow servant in the castle? Who was it, Mindy?"

She is doing this well, thought the Sergeant. In the end you can't beat the gentry for putting sharp questions. It must be in the blood. We could do with her as well as Mindy, could the Major and I. What a team we should make.

"So who is this servant?" Fanny asked, her voice severe. "Come, Mindy. Answer."

"Tom Tinker, he is very short, and therefore loves to talk so that you will be his friend."

"And who's servant is he?"

"Lord Frederic's. Lord Frederic Bertie."

Both women turned to look at Sergeant Denny.

"Yes," he said. "It is Lord Frederic who is murdered. I found him. I knew his face."

"He was killed for being what he was," said Mindy.

"No," said the Sergeant. "He was killed for being a woman. Don't go out into the streets."

Before they could speak again there was sound feet clipping down the stone corridors.

Round the corner came two men: Winter Ames and James Manston. Neither man looked as well groomed as usual, in fact Winter Ames had not put on gloves and wore no hat, and Manston looked unwell.

"And how are you? How are you?" said Manston. "We have been so concerned, Miss Fanny, since we heard of the new killing. The villain, the villain."

Fanny drew her robe about her more closely and spoke with dignity. "Thank you, but I cannot receive you now. Charlotte will talk to you and take a message," she bowed and retreated into her room.

In a low voice Winter Ames addressed himself to Mindy. "What are we to say, except that we fear the violence in the town, there is an atmosphere... it would be better to stay out of it. The infection too... but that gets everywhere." He looked towards Manston as if he feared for him. "I want to protect you and Miss Burney." To himself, he was saying: "I believe I am now in love with Miss Burney, but yet I am strongly drawn to this woman here." He looked into Mindy's bright, keen eyes.

"Did you know Lord Frederic?" Mindy asked.

Ames hesitated, still looking at his companion who was mopping his brow. "Yes, he came into the theatre often." Again he hesitated. "We knew his ways, of course. Once or twice he asked if he could take part of one of our plays... he asked to play Viola in *Twelfth Night*. Not possible, of course, he could speak the poetry, I daresay, but there is more to it than that. In addition to which he could have been at least six inches taller than his supposed twin... You know the play?"

Mindy nodded. She did not but it did not matter.

"Manston lent him stage costumes once or twice, unwise, I thought, but there you are. Mercifully, he did not wear one when he died."

—Looking for rough trade that's why, thought the Sergeant who was listening.

"But he was harmless, poor fellow, and did not deserve to die the way he did."

"It will cause a great scandal," pontificated Manston, with some satisfaction, the Sergeant thought. "Except the Court will sit on it, and all will be suppressed."

Sergeant Denny, who had been observing and listening all with alert interest, bowed to the two men. "Sergeant Denny at your service, sirs," introducing himself, since no one else seemed about to do it. Then he bowed again to Mindy: "Your servant, Miss Minden," after which he swung on his heel and marched down the corridor.

His thoughts were interesting to him. What a pair, he summed up. I am not sure what I make of them. I like one more than t'other.

As he rounded the sharp bend of the corridor, he was passed by a stout, hurrying figure which he recognised as one of the Queen's messengers, by name Sam Pillby.

Sam was muttering as he ran: "His Majesty wishes to see you, Miss Burney, but he is sick and her Majesty says you are not to come. On no account are you come to His

GWENDOLINE BUTLER

Majesty however so much he should send to ask... Not to come, not to come," he was muttering as he ran.

"Well, that's interesting too," thought the Sergeant. Actors and messengers and the King, all after Miss Fanny. Now that's a conglomeration. He was pleased with that word and said again to himself as he walked to where they had their chambers.

To Major Mearns, when he got back to their rooms, where the Major was smoking while he read *The Times*, he said: "What do you think about actors?"

The Major did not raise his head from his reading: "Kittle cattle," he murmured over his pipe. "So what did you find out when you were out walking. You found a dead body, you knew the victim, Anything else? No, then out you go and find out something more. It is all out there waiting."

"And can wait while you sit there reading," said Denny, putting himself comfortably into a chair by the fire and helping himself to some of the Major's wine. Red and comforting it was to a troubled man, as a good vintage should be. Out of the royal cellars through a back route. So much there, never be missed, He refilled his glass. "How's your grandmother?" he said as he drank.

"I heard what you say, and my grandmother, if she is still alive will be over one hundred years, but it is my belief, or so I was led to believe that she died before I was born. And don't punish the claret."

He stood, a commanding figure when he chose. "You go out and collect information and I do the thinking."

"Yes, Major. I'm always the foot soldier, am I?"

"No, I go out on little forays of my own."

The Sergeant slapped his leg and let out a gale of laughter. "I knew it, I knew it. I knew you did not get your information from the stars."

"I went to the Marly."

"Ah."

163

THE KING CRIED MURDER!

The Marlborough Arms was a drinking house with good ales and a good wine if you wanted it. You could get a simple hot meal as well. Nothing fine or fancy but all cleanly served and tasty. It had a great following, not all of it totally respectable. All were welcome by mine host, John Tarten and Bess his wife, and they were a pair who knew how to keep the peace in the Marly.

The comfortable atmosphere and the good drink loosened tongues, a fact that Major Mearns and Sergeant Denny knew full well. Major Mearns in particular made good use of this.

The Major had a way of becoming almost invisible, of being there and yet with no notice taken of him, a gift from the heavens quite remarkable in a man of his size and which Denny could not emulate.

"You stand out like a sore thumb, Denny," the Major said to him once, half amused, half irritated. "A blind, deaf man could not forget you were there."

"They get wind of me," Denny had answered sadly. "I smell wrong." He did smoke a particularly powerful tobacco and also took snuff.

"I took it that I might see our old friend Tossy there."

Tossy had a peculiar part in Windsor society which the Sergeant always found difficult to understand. There was no understanding Tossy.

It was believed that his full name was William Star, but he came from the village of Tosser St Mary, near Windsor and seemed to be called after the village. The origin of the name Tosser was lost in antiquity but it was believed that it derived from the old English owner of the estate, dispossessed by the Norman but living on in the name of the village. It might even be that he had left descendants and that Tossy, whose reasons for leaving the village were obscure and probably not honourable, was one of them.

What he had done with his life since was a mystery: certainly he had served in the army, learning military terms and how to drink like a Trojan. If he had picked up no discipline, he had learned a certain knack in domestic matters so that he could, if sober, tidy a room, make a bed and cook a simple meal. Aye and eat it too, as one employer had complained. With all these skills he worked as a houseman for the Poor Knights of Windsor, military pensioners living in the Castle wards.

Tossy had other jobs, mysterious, probably criminous, and moved in a kind of underworld in which many things were done and known about. Certain it was that he had seen the inside of more than one prison or House of Correction, but it was conjectured that even there he had been on good terms with the warders and earned himself an extra pint of ale while even his fellow prisoners had a kind of grumbling friendliness for him. He was not trustworthy but was trusted. In short, a man whom most called his own worst enemy.

"Tossy, eh? He'll drink himself to death one day," commented Denny.

"Likely enough." He stirred himself enough to add: "He confirms that it is town gossip that the King is mad, that while mad he talks about women and love-making in no uncertain terms and complains about the Queen. He is also said to 'escape' sometimes. And there are tales of large figure seen in the back streets of the town in white, but no one has seen the face and although they joke it is His Majesty, no one has seen his face. Likewise, there is a tall figure seemingly dressed like the King, white britches, red coat, orders. No crown, they joke. But Tossy has not seen him on the streets of Windsor, nor does he know anyone who has, but it is always the next person or that person's friend."

"So it is all tales? Might be true, for all that."

The Major shrugged. "What is interesting is that Miss

Burney's name comes in, she is named, His Majesty is interested in her, it is known."

"There is always gossip about the King and his Court... usually about the Prince of Wales," said Denny, dryly. "And we must remember that Miss Burney is famous in her right as a celebrated author. We should not forget it."

"Tossy and his circle are not likely to be great readers."

"True." Denny had not read the novel *Evelina*; the daily newspaper was his only reading material. But to his surprise, at that moment, he saw a copy of the novel on the table by the Major.

"I am trying it," said Mearns, sheepishly. "I have heard that James Manston is trying to make a play of it."

Since Major Mearns seemed willing to relapse into silence, Denny gave him another prod. "I suppose he knew Lord Frederic Bertie?"

"He did. And his way of life was known. But Tossy says he never before dressed up as a poor woman, preferring to deck himself up in rich silks and soft muslins. He thinks he had a new lover, perhaps a boatman, or a poor soldier from the barracks."

"He was a bit of an actor," said Denny thoughtfully.

"Or even a rich man who liked a touch of the dirt..." continued the Major.

"What a world we live in," said Denny thoughtfully. "Did he have a name?" Tossy could usually point the finger if you paid him enough.

"No name. Although he was hinting that there was someone connected with Lord Frederic whose name he could give me if he dared."

"Dared?" That did not sound like Tossy, who, in a subterranean way, dared much.

"A person of position, is the guess, I made."

"Someone from the Court?"

"It could be so. Or a magistrate, or a doctor, or a high

GWENDOLINE BUTLER

ranking officer from the barracks. He dare not name
higher; there is a law of treason which Tossy fears if he
fears nothing else. I am not sure if there is anything in it."
The Major shrugged. "The town gossip is that the killer of
Lord Frederic is the same who killed the other women."

"I am of the same mind," said Denny.

"Whether the two characters are one and the same and
the person of position is also the murderer of women, is
something the town gossips are still puzzling over. It would
amuse them if so. Agreeable to have a high and mighty on
the gallows. Or would the executioner's axe be called in,
they ask."

"So Tossy gave you nothing hard about the killer?"

The Major grinned. "He would like it to be either the
King or the Prince of Wales, but he is not hopeful of it."

"But I would not say he gave nothing: he thinks the killer
and Lord Fred knew each other, that in the moment of dying, the Lord Frederic recognised his killer."

"Why should Tossy think this?"

For a moment, Major Mearns was silent. "You found the
body, did you not see that each eye had been pierced with
the knife?"

"I saw the punctures," Denny said quietly. "And I know
there is a common superstition that the image of the killer
is imprinted on the eyeball in death."

He did not enjoy the picture of that act of recognition in
the moment of death.

Nor the idea that Lord Frederic had known his killer.

Into the moment of silence, the Major said: "But I did
not come away with nothing at all. Tossy gave me a name:
Nicholas Larkin, and an address 2, Lower Bell Yard."

Denny looked at him: Lower Bell Yard was not the best
of addresses nor was number 2 the best house in it. An
overcrowded slum where the poorest lived, jammed in
together, men, women and children, often sharing beds,

167

one set in the day and another at night. Windsor was spared the worst of the rookeries which London knew but it had its own horrors.

"Larkin may have been the man that Lord Frederic was on the way to meet."

"And also his killer?"

"That is what we must try to find out."

Lower Bell Yard was never quiet but it was always dark at night. No braziers burned to light the passer-by. The inhabitants preferred the dark. Nor were there passers-by, no one came this way after the sun had gone down if they could avoid it.

Although no one was about except a mangy dog and a thin cat with a rat in her mouth, that did not meant the arrival of Mearns and Denny went unobserved.

Old Mother Markie who lived in the basement of the first house in Lower Bell Yard saw their feet and knew by the bright polish of the Major's boots that he was a stranger. Not the sort of feet that usually came down the Yard.

Polly Pinkus who dwelt in an attic (along with six other people and the odd baby) looked down and saw the two men. She did not know them, but knew them for unlikely strangers. Ladies, beshawled and carrying a basket with perhaps a manservant in tow, came down the Yard sometimes on charitable missions of soup and old clothes. For these visitors of mercy, Polly felt a mixture of anger and amusement. Gratitude, she did not feel. Why should she feel grateful for broken vittles and old clothes, she could thieve better and she knew it. Like an angry mongrel she would bite the hand that fed her if she could. Her head ached and something raged inside her so perhaps she was ill.

On the floor behind her something wailed.

"Your kid's crying, Polly," said a voice. "Terrible wail it's got. I think it's poorly."

168

"I dessay," Polly answered. "We all are, as far as I see."

The cry of the baby stopped. "He'll die," she said without emotion. "Dr Seaton said he wouldn't last out the week. Mine never last the year out."

"Lucky you are to have a doctor," said another voice. "Even if he looks more like an animal, dressed up in that black robe, as he goes around. Still, you have that luck."

Polly laughed not with much humour. "Lucky, is it?"

"He calls me a Demonstration, but I do not know of what, unless it be never to have anything and always to be wanting."

She went back to looking out of the window. The two men had disappeared into number 2.

In that house, Mary Diggens was behind her door, listening to the arrival of the two men.

They had pushed open the front door which was never locked, the key having been long since lost, and she could hear their voices.

She listened.

"The gentlemen are shouting for you, Jack," she said.

From his bed on the floor, Larkin told her to let them in then.

But they were already pushing open the door. Larkin was rolled up in a blanket on the floor, Mary Diggens was nursing the baby, and her younger children were playing on the floor. Also on the floor was a tabby scratching its fleas.

"Jack Larkin?"

He rolled over in his blankets, sat up and looked at them. A handsome, haggard young face, unshaven but clean beneath the beard.

He looked thin and tired and hungry.

"You want me, sirs?"

There was an impudent note in his voice.

"We would like to speak to you."

"Speak you may but I cannot rise up to greet you because I have nought on but my britches... but if it pleases your lordships, I will rise up to give you pleasure."

"Jack, Jack," protested his landlady, who seemed as aware of the innuendo as the Major and Sergeant themselves.

A plain, gentle woman who appeared to bear no resentment to a life which had presented her with a numerous family, an absent husband, and a lodger with whom she was not at ease.

"But, your lordships, I like to be paid for my troubles."

"He's a wicked boy." This was a new voice, shrill and old.

The Major turned to a dark corner of the room where what he had taken to be a bundle of rags turned out to have a face and voice.

"Mother Kay, be quiet," said Mrs Diggens, moved at last to make a protest.

"A man must make a living," said the insolent boy. "What have I got to sell? Guess for yourselves, my lords, and if you have to come to bargain, I say that for two of you the price is more than doubled. Has to be, a body can only do so much. You must take turns or go at both together."

The Major was making deep noises in his throat of anger.

"He has rumbled us," said Denny.

"I know who you are."

"Did Lord Frederic tell you then?"

Jack Larkin rose out of his bed, wrapping the ragged blanket round him. "Get us a drink of water, Molly girl," he said to Mary Diggens.

Mary looked at him without a word, then took a mug and went to a tap on the landing outside.

When she came back with a tin mug full, he downed it in a gulp.

"I am for the rough trade, sir." He said, his voice, angry,

170

defiant. "Do I enjoy it? To the hilt, sir, to the hilt."

"I take the allusion, my man," said the Major.

"Your man I am not, Major. Not without you pay me."

He was, Denny thought, in the after stage of great drinking, when your body thirsts, but you are not yet in your right mind.

"You know me?"

"Aye, and the Sergeant too. You do everything in pairs." An insult was meant but not taken.

Mary Diggens gave a wail of protest.

"And you need say nothing, Mary Diggens, we all know how you earn a penny when Miss Burney does not call with food. Or when you fancy a nip of gin."

A shriek from the corner burst forth at him.

"Oh we all know that you too like to sup the gin, mother." He did not turn his head to look at her and ignored the eldritch mutter that came from the corner.

Were they one family of old mother, daughter and son, Denny asked himself, or just the flotsam and jetsam of society thrown together? He thought the latter; he had seen enough of the world of poverty to know that it made for strange fellowships.

"Tell me about Lord Frederic," said the Major, looking around for a chair. There were none, so he leaned against the wall.

Denny remained upright, and stiffened his shoulders. He would not put Jack past attacking them. But he did not. He took water, drank it down.

"Why should I speak of him? Let him do it for himself."

"Lord Frederic is dead. Stabbed."

"You lie." Larkin choked on the words.

"No."

Jack Larkin got up to walk about the room; he was struggling to control his emotions. At last he swung round and faced Mearns and Denny.

"It was not my doing."

Mearns did not answer. He was inclined to believe Larkin.

"We understood each other, he paid me and I served his wants. It was an arrangement."

"Did you have such an arrangement with other men?"

Jack shrugged. "A man must live." He looked about him. "Not in much comfort, I admit, but at least not on the streets. I hope to go to London, I believe I should do better there. Lord Frederic would have helped me, he had friends there he would introduce me to."

"You'd need a new suit of clothes," said the old woman in the corner.

Larkin ignored her. "I can't believe Lord Frederic is dead. Was it in duel between gentlemen?"

"He was murdered in an alley," said Mearns bluntly.

The old woman let out a scream. "We shall all be murdered."

"Don't take any notice of her, she enjoys a sensation. Good luck if she is killed, we won't miss her."

"There's a good Christian man for you," shrieked the old woman.

The Major touched Larkin on the arm, and spoke in a low voice. "Come to the door, I want to talk to you without the other two hearing."

"What is it you want?" But Larkin moved towards the door.

"Was it Lord Frederic's habit to dress up as a woman?"

"Ay. It was a game that amused him. He had more than one brocades and embroidered silks."

Mearns gave an interested look at Denny, "What about the clothes of a poor woman, did he use them?"

Larkin frowned. "How poor?"

"Ragged, torn garments, no silks or laces."

"No, I never saw such on him... But I know he wandered the streets after dark when in the mood, and then, I daresay he did not wear fine clothes."

"Did he go out just to meet anyone or was it a person he knew?"

Larkin shook his head. "Do you suppose he confided in such as me?"

"How did he arrange to meet you?"

Larkin hesitated, then said: "I would walk on the Lower Road by the river and he would join me there if he so desired."

"And if he did not come?"

"I had other contacts."

"Of which you will say nothing?"

Larkin shrugged.

"And where did Lord Frederic meet these other men?"

"Dark people in dark places," was the enigmatic reply.

Silently the Major admitted to himself that it was in such a place his lordship's body had been found.

"What do you make of Larkin?" he asked as they left.

"Truthful enough granted his way of life," Denny said grudgingly. "I think he liked his lordship well enough. Lord Frederic was a provider, not one he would kill, even if he was a killer which I think he is not."

"Lord Frederic was living a dangerous life. I wonder if he had been attacked before?"

"Likely enough. And come through unscathed. He was a big strong man and would expect to get the better of an encounter." That's the aristocracy for you, thought Denny, always expect to be the winners.

Except that according to his grandmother Lord Frederic was not a true aristocrat.

They walked towards the Castle in silence, both thinking, Denny surprisingly aware that he would miss Lord

Frederic, whom perhaps he had not liked but who had flashes of wit and attraction that drew you towards him, willy nilly.

Before they got to the Castle, the Major said: "I want to see the street where you found Lord Frederic."

Tumble Alley had been tidied up before they got there and was empty, not even the town constable left.

"Was there any blood on the stones?" asked Mearns, looking about him.

"There is some still." Denny pointed to a small patch of dark red near the gunner where it had drained. "And there was some on the King's handkerchief on his shirt too, I think." He had caught a glimpse of something.

"Kings shouldn't have blood on them," said Mearns.

"It will be washed away by now."

"Impossible to question the King," Mearns said, his face grim.

"But Silverline might get something from him. Or even Lord Somerton. He talks to those two if to anyone. And might talk to Miss Burney if in the mood."

"Silverline would never betray the King, nor would Edward Somerton. They might tell the Queen, but they would never tell us."

They halted in the middle of the alley, stopped by the enormity of questioning His Majesty about murder. There could be no doubt that in his madness the King would think of it as lawful execution of his subjects and not murder.

"If not the King, then whom? Windsor is not a big city. We should be able to get a wind of this wandering killer. Someone must suspect him."

They walked on down the alley, studying the road, the gutters and the walls of the building that lined it. Mearns asked what they were and Denny told him that one was a warehouse and the other a small brewery. The walls were brick with no windows so there would have been no observers.

The gutter that ran down the middle of the alley was filled with rubbish.

Mearns bent down and picked up a piece of paper. "Rubbish. A theatre favour. And next to it a hank of fair hair," He picked it up to study. "I think Lord Frederic must have torn it out of his killer's hair as he bent over him."

"Could he do that?" queried Denny.

"Yes, certainly, I think, in the desperate act of dying."

"So we look for a man who has lost a lock of hair?"

"Fair hair," said the Major thoughtfully. "Fine fair hair."

Denny was studying it with interest: "But there is no blood on it, no roots, that is strange. Perhaps he does not bleed, this man who kills." He put the hank of hair in his pocket. "I shall keep this; objects can talk too."

ELEVEN

The murder of Lord Frederic, with its accompanying details of his dress, and how he was murdered (they did not have to explain why to that sophisticated audience) was soon the main topic of conversation in the Castle. It took over from anxious discussion of the new pink spot ailment, which had already penetrated the Castle's defences, laying low several courtiers. It had already crept into the royal nurseries causing the Queen some anxiety. The Royal Pair had a large and healthy family, probably a larger family than they might have desired, and they feared to see them sicken one by one. As it was, the two youngest, one girl and a boy were ill with the spot.

The Head Nurse, Lady Beeston was of the opinion the whole nursery should pack up and go to the palace at Kew taking the sick with them. But the doctors, in solemn conclave, forbade this, saying that the two poor sick little creatures must not be moved. Although, as Lady Beeston said, they might have been as warm and comfortable in the wagonette on the way to Kew as in their own beds.

Her Majesty was equally anxious to send the King off to Kew, but there the cause was his erratic behaviour. She had heard of the murders, everyone had done, but she closed her mind to any connection with the King.

All the same, she did not like the keen interest he took in all particulars relating to the deaths. "It is not how you should be, my dear," she said to him solemnly. "This is not being the King."

But since the doctors would not let the Queen leave Windsor, or so she claimed, the King would not go without her.

Fanny thought the Queen would be very glad to have the King depart to Kew and leave her in Windsor, it struck her that the Queen longed silently for solitude. But it was not to be. They must all go or none at all.

So plans were made that they would go as soon as the little Prince and Princess had recovered.

Fanny supposed that she would have to go too. The Queen knew that she had gone into the town with some simple medicines and supplies to do some nursing. This Her Majesty did not approve of.

"Your first duty is to Us," she said to Fanny. Not severely, she was in many ways a gentle woman, but certainly with the full sense of what was owed to her position from such as Fanny. Indeed, Fanny thought, she was probably surprised that she had to say it.

Not that it stopped Fanny; it only made her exits from the Castle more discreet. It was very hard to be secretive in the Castle, there were so many eyes always watching, but with Mindy's help she managed it twice or thrice.

Sergeant Denny had warned the two young women to be careful because it seemed the unknown killer was getting more reckless; Winter Ames also urged caution.

He came to call one evening to enquire after their health and warn against the dangers of Windsor at the moment. He arrived after Fanny had dressed the Queen and was free.

On her way back through the corridors and down the

big staircases she had had the uneasy sense that she was watched, that someone followed behind. She swung once or twice but could see no one and decided it was her imagination. There were so many dark corners in the castle. But it made her listen to the Sergeant's words of warning.

"Because if a strong man like Lord Frederic can be felled, so could a weak woman." Then he corrected himself and said quickly. "I mean a tender woman."

Fanny was willing to be a tender woman although in Mindy's face she saw a keen refusal. No, Mindy would not be tender. Ladies could be tender; it was for Mindy to be hard and adroit.

When Winter had gone, she said to Mindy: "He is anxious to be protective. I think New England gentlemen do stand guard over their womenfolk."

"I thought they sent them out to chop down trees and build wooden houses."

"There may have been something of that sort in the beginning," Fanny said. "But not, I fancy any longer."

Mindy had her own question: "What would you do if you met the murderer and saw his knife?"

"Run if I could, and scream for help. I have a good loud voice," she added: "I must own I should like to see his face."

That's the gentle lady, thought Mindy with some irony, but they can always do and dare more than you think.

"I thought I heard someone behind me as I came from the Queen," said Fanny in a wary voice, looking to see what reaction she could from Mindy.

"And was there anyone?"

"I didn't see anyone. It was just a sensation."

"But you think there was someone?"

Fanny nodded. "I did then. Now I am not so sure. In

the Castle... we must be safe here."

There was a hammering on the door and the Sergeant was back. "Have you been killing a cat?" he demanded at once.

"Of course not," said Mindy. "Why?"

"There's blood on the floor. And a smear on the wall."

Mindy came out to look where the Sergeant was standing. Along the wall she could see a thin streak of dark red which looked as though a finger had traced it there. On the floor below was another smear, this time as if a foot had left it there.

Fanny came to the door behind her. "What is it?"

"Come to look for yourself."

Fanny examined the traces, holding up a candle for a better viewing. "It's very little."

"Enough," said Denny. "I think it has been deliberately left here."

"Is the blood from poor Lord Frederic?"

"I can't tell... there may be another body, lying, hidden."

"You are frightening me," said Fanny, glad that Mindy was by her side.

"I mean to, miss. You must be on your guard."

"The likes of Miss Burney don't get murdered," said Mindy stoutly.

"We are all at risk," was what Denny said, and repeated it to himself as he trudged back to where the Major sat by his fire.

The Major raised his head from his newspaper. "So you have been out frightening the young ladies."

"Not much frightens Mindy," answered Denny. "And Miss Burney is frightened which I think is right and proper, for there was blood, put there on purpose, I believe, sir, on the wall and floor near Miss Burney's room. Not much, but there to see if you looked."

The Major stood up and walked around the room. "I had a message from Mr Pitt ordering me to offer what help I could to the Magistrate and his officers. I shall do that, of course, but I would rather we worked on our own for Sir George is a bumbling man, and his officers worse."

Denny had already noticed that the Major had no opinion of Sir George, he had not much himself but thought that the good baronet had a certain shrewdness that might be serviceable.

"We shall have to show him some courtesy," went Mearns. "We had better call. He is proud of that great, raw, square house he built for himself."

"He is rich then?"

"Trade. Sugar. His father made the money in the City first and Sir George has improved on it. He has six children, all boys, so it will be soon spent unless he sends them all to sea as some do."

Many fine families were dispersed to the navy or to the colonies. Not all the sons returned.

"The new pink spot may provide for them," said Denny cynically. He allowed the Major to pour him some wine which he sat sipping while thinking. Then he rose to his feet.

"We aren't off to see Sir George yet," protested Mearns. "He will still be at the card table and not to be disturbed."

There was a Gentlemen's Club below the castle where the local gentry met to play cards and drink and gossip. The Major went there himself to pick up the news of the day and learn the scandals of the town, although he gambled but little and hated to lose. Nevertheless he relished being a member of the KitKat Club (the name copied from a famous London original) and paid his dues on demand.

"No, Major, there is something I must do before we go."

Denny let himself out of their almost subterranean set of rooms where you could only see the castle grounds by standing to stare out of the high set window.

He had his hand on the door handle when the Major said: "Before you go, tell me what you make of this killer. Is he a rough fellow that may soon be caught?"

Denny shook his head. "He shows some skill in selecting his victims. Not one has called out when attacked. Or if there has been a shout, then it has not been heard. This man is clever enough. As for manners and education, that I cannot say. But I would make a guess that he has a pretty manner when he likes and does not alarm his prey."

"Lord Frederic was a good strong fellow, and could have defended himself," mused the Major.

"Died without a struggle as far as I could see," said the Major. "There is something about this killer that hides what he is planning."

"Yes, I believe you."

"I wonder if Lord Frederic knew him, if they had arranged to meet," mused the Major. "Don't tell me his lordship went out dressed like that with no plan in his head. No, he was aiming to meet someone and that someone killed him. Where did he change? Do you know? He never walked through the castle dressed like that."

"There are plenty of dark back passages, which I daresay he knew of. With covering over his head, he might have flitted through without anyone being much the wiser. I expect he had done it more than once."

"Likely, likely." And the Major settled back in his chair with his wine. "Get on with what you want then, Sergeant, but come back to me here."

Denny paced down the long dark corridor looking to right and left where there were various small pantries and lobbies, now empty and dusty. None were in daily use, but all had both a purpose in the past and the prospect of one to come. One day, Denny thought, perhaps in a new reign, a fresh hand would fall upon these cubby holes and they would be cleaned, painted and given a fresh use. They had names such as Lord Franklin's Pantry, the Canterbury Corner, Alfred's sink, these names were used even if their origins were long forgotten.

Denny took a quick look inside each little place, smelt the air, found nothing of interest and passed on, up the staircase to the next corridor.

Here too were small rooms and on this floor they had some use with furniture and packing cases stared in some of them. At the end of the corridor, before it led to where Fanny Burney had her rooms, was Dookey's Nook.

Who Dookey was and what went on in his nook, Denny did not know.

He looked in each as he passed. Dookey's Nook was dark and silent as the other closets. But he put his head into the door, and he smelt humanity.

Someone had been in there.

A man, he knew that at once, a man who smoked and used scent. The scent he did not recognise but it was not cheap. Not the sort that you could buy off a stall in Windsor market-place, wrapped in gaudy paper. This scent had come from London, from one of those shops in Bond Street that decked out men.

Denny did not use scent himself but he had had a young officer in India who had always showered himself with it, and he had learnt to know quality when he smelt it. You needed to be rich to use this scent, he thought. Or else, very very fond of yourself.

THE KING CRIED MURDER!

"Stinks like Lieutenant Champeneys," he murmured to himself. That poor young officer had died in India, killed in an action of no consequence. He had been buried there with Denny among the bearers. Not the only man to die then, but the youngest and the richest.

His ghost came back to stand by Denny's side as he went into Dookey's Nook. The ghost performed his correct function of telling the Sergeant what he should not do: ghosts should always warn, tell you what not to do, and never what you should do. Here the ghost of Lieutenant Champeneys warned him not to stamp into Dookey's Nook without a light. It might be dangerous.

He went back to where the Major was still smoking.

"Back already?"

"I need a light."

The Major raised an eyebrow.

"I want to look in Dookey's Nook." Denny took the candle that stood on the table. "Someone has been there. May be there now, for all I know."

Major Mearns got to his feet. "Then I shall come too. You are rash and impetuous at times, Denny."

The Sergeant did not accept this judgement but now was not the time to say so.

As soon as they came into Dookey's Nook, the Major took up the mantle of the ghostly Lieutenant and began to tell Denny what he should not do.

"Hold the light steady and do not let the candle drip." The Major looked around him. The pantry ran back into the castle wall and had probably been there since the Norman builders laid the wall with Dookey's Nook as part of it.

At some point in its history it had been used to store china, possibly the Dook's china for the dusty blue and white china plates and dishes which rested in piles on the shelves looked as if they might have been brought back from some campaign as the spoils of victory.

Two great ewers rested on the dusty floor. Behind deep bowls of plain, thick white china were stacked in rows. It was just possible to see a faint crest through the dirt.

"I suppose this is Dooky's china, whoever Dooky was," mused the Major as he looked around him. "Yes, you are right, someone has been in here, I can smell him. The scent and behind it a body. A man." He bent his head: "What are you doing down there, Denny?"

Sergeant Denny was kneeling on the floor where he was examining some rags and crumpled paper. "This is where he stood and this is what he did."

"When you make mysteries, Denny, I don't care for it. Make clear what you mean."

And by way of finding out for himself, the Major got down on the floor too. He picked up one of the rags and sniffed it. "Blood," he said.

"He brought the bloody rags here that he smeared on the floor and wall near Miss Burney's room. He hid in here till he could do the job. Not many people pass this way, so he would not have waited long."

"This killer is mad," said Mearns, getting to his feet.

"But full of enjoyment. He stood here waiting, full of pleasure. If pleasure smelt, we would smell it." Denny too got to his feet. "He stood here like an executioner."

"I don't like what you say."

"If it's the King, he won't go to Tyburn." He gathered up the bloodied rags and the papers. "But no, the King does not wear scent... the Prince of Wales now..."

The Major glared at Denny. "No jokes."

No jokes indeed, thought Denny.

"Is the killer, whoever he may be, in the Castle now? Is that your opinion?"

"Sir, I do not know where our executioner is, in the

castle or on the streets, but I think he is looking for a new victim. He is not satisfied."

There was a sound of running footsteps, both men looked up to see Mindy coming down the stairs.

"I hoped I would find you here, you were seen coming this way, you are not so easily hidden," she said, getting her breath back. "While I was in the upper pantry, one of the Queen's maids came in. Eliza Gage. She is a friend, and seeing she looked flustered, I asked her what was wrong and she told me: the King is missing."

"How do they know?" asked the Major.

"When his valet and his gentlemen went to dress him for this evening, he was not to be found. A search is going on. Miss Burney is with the Queen, what she learns, she will tell me. The Queen trusts her."

"And where were you running to?" asked the Major.

"I was coming to tell you."

"Now we know," said the Major, "and what are we to do about it?"

For a moment they stood in silence, then the quiet was broken by the sound of laughter.

Laughter floating up the stairs from the flight below. Then feet stamping up towards them.

Someone who laughed and was heavy footed.

"The King," said Denny.

There he was, trudging along the corridor towards them, a laugh bursting forth every so often.

A right royal, mad laugh, and the look on the face not the sanest either.

King George advanced up the stairs towards the trio, laughing. "Here I am, here I am. You are glad to see me, your King. Salute me." Blood dropped from his arm, "Damme, I am always cutting myself. Did you see my shirt yesterday?" He was mopping up with his handkerchief. "Salute me, damn you."

The men did so hastily.

They did not fail to notice that he had a long sharp knife in his left hand. There was a streak of blood on his nightshirt.

"Salute me," he said in a loud voice.

The men did as commanded once again.

"The young woman too."

Mindy sketched a salute. And then she curtsied. Better get it right, both ways.

The King roared with laughter, came up to her and bussed her. He was wearing a red long coat with military frogging over a long white robe. The Garter Star rested on his chest and the blue sash that went with it was draped across what was clearly, on a closer look, his night robe.

He was a cheerful mess.

"Stand by, stand guard," he commanded. "This is your monarch talking to you."

Then he started to roar again. Words were not easy to pick out, but Denny thought he was ordering them, all three, to march with them.

He could see by the look on Mindy's face that she would be ready to join in.

But the King did not wait for them, he turned round, gave another roar, and was off down the staircase in the direction whence he had come.

"After him," ordered the Major, already beginning to run. The King was already disappearing, laughing and roaring as he did so.

Down the staircase they tumbled, the Sergeant and Mindy the quickest. Behind them, they could hear not only the Major stumbling along, but other feet as well. The hunt for the King was on.

At the bottom of the staircase, they saw the red and white figure just disappearing out of view, with the ghost of a laugh following.

By the time Mindy, who was fleetest of foot, got to the end of the corridor, there was no sign of the King.

Mindy let the Sergeant and the Major catch her up. Behind, came several of the gentlemen of the Royal Household.

"His Majesty grew up in the Castle, he was a boy here, of course he knew the passages and secret ways out," said Major Mearns.

"You should have caught His Majesty," said one of his gentleman when he had stopped panting. This was Sir Harry Throckmorton, one of his longest serving gentlemen. He had been with the King in the schoolroom, and was now as thickset and grey haired as his master. He was married to one of the Queen's Ladies in Waiting.

"There was no catching him," said Mindy.

Sir Harry had been joined by two other gentlemen of the chamber, one Mr William Place was younger than his companion, Captain, the Honourable Edward Evelyn. Mr Place was silent but Captain Evelyn never stopped talking: "What a thing, what a thing," he said, over and over again. "What a thing..."

"T'isn't the first time the King has been on the run," said Mindy.

Captain Evelyn did not answer her, did not even look at her, for him, such as Mindy did not exist.

"Does the Queen know?" she went on.

She was answered by patter of feet on the stairs together with the rustle of thick, stiff silk.

Here was Queen Charlotte, in a dark blue silk gown. Diamonds in her ears, pearls hanging about her throat. Behind her walked Mrs Schellenbarter, dressed in black, and behind her came Fanny Burney. Fanny wore pale muslin.

"Where is His Majesty?" Her accent was more pronouncedly German than usual. "He must be found. You must find him. It is your duty." She tapped her foot impatiently.

Captain Evelyn bowed. "Ma'am." He saluted and swung on his heel, marching down the corridor in the direction in which the King had disappeared. Sir Harry and William Place hesitated, then fell in behind him.

Her Majesty stayed for a moment till they were out of sight, then walked back up the stairs, followed by Mrs Schellenbarter and Fanny.

"The King will soon by found, running through the streets like that," was Mindy's frank opinion, "Red jacket, Garter Star, he will be known at once."

"Not the same as catching him," said Denny. "He can run fast."

Major Mearns said that he did not think the men who had run after the King wanted to catch him, not to lay strong hands on him and drag him back. They would take care to be gentle with him. Treason, after all, to treat the King's person with violence, he ended.

He offered his opinion: "I think the King will not leave the Castle... he may run into the Park."

"No, he will get out into the town, if he can, I could see it in his face." said Denny. "Unless the Guard is called out. Perhaps even then." He had a momentary vision of the His Majesty racing through the town followed by his Court and the immensely respectful Guard. All, no doubt, aware that he bore a knife, ready to use on them. His lips twitched. "Oh poor King George, he will never be free. That is why he is mad, it is his only way of escape."

"He is seriously mad," said the Major. "You saw the knife. I shall be obliged to tell Mr Pitt."

"And will you say he might be a killer?"

"Yes," said the Major, "I must. He knows about the madness... many will have told, he has seen for himself. But the murders... He must be told, Lord Frederic was a friend."

Their eyes met. And more than a friend, possibly.

"If the King had blood on him," said Denny. "I believe it was his own where he stabbed himself. I saw a long bloody trail on his right arm."

"It's a bad business, a bad business." The Major was walking back to their rooms. "I must write a report for Mr Pitt."

The Major had a messenger of whom he made full use, sending reports not only to the Prime Minister but also the London *Times*. Jack Scroggs was waiting for him in his room, a short bent figure with a lively face.

"Thought you'd want me, sir."

"Aye, Jack. Sit you down and wait while I write."

Scroggs had served with the Major and Sergeant Denny, losing the sight of one eye on campaign, but he made excellent use of the one remaining. Denny knew that odd snippets of information and gossip filtered through him and hence to London. He was as useful to the Major as the gossips of the KitKat Club.

He had something to say now.

"I hear Lord Frederic had a little circle of playmates in London, it might be an idea to talk to them."

"Do you know their names.?"

"Mr Pitt will know them," said Jack Scroggs slyly. "He is one of them."

Mearns did not allow Scroggs too much freedom. "They were at Eton together," he said.

Scroggs said nothing, but his silence indicated what he thought of Eton.

"Lord Fred's taste was for simple men," he allowed after a pause while the Major was writing.

"Shut up, Scroggs."

The letter finished, he handed it to his messenger, and ordered him to take it to Westminster straight and to wait for a reply. "Take the grey mare, she is fast."

Scroggs saluted and hobbled out. In spite of his appearance he was a good horseman. He had ridden the grey mare before and thought well of her.

"You trust that man," said Denny.

"I do." The Major added grimly: "He knows if he betrayed me that he would be out on a transport off to Australia before he could speak."

"He's got a wife in Windsor," observed Denny. "Did you know? He has one in London too."

"I don't suppose that is the end of it. He always has a wife or two, he left one behind in India. He calls them wives, whether he marries them or not, I am not sure."

There came a rap on the door, and Jack Scroggs presented himself again. "I forgot to tell you, Major Mearns, that Dr Seaton asked to see the body of Lord Frederic. He called on the Magistrate and asked permission. I thought it was something you should know." His voice was rough and eager.

"How do you know this?"

"My wife works for Sir George, she does the laundry. She heard them talking... she has worked for Dr Seaton too."

"And she listened, I suppose?"

"Sir George has a loud voice."

"And did he say why he asked?"

"To examine the body, sir. To see how he was killed and how it compared with other killings. Also to see if Lord Frederic was a proper man, sir. His organs, sir."

"And did Sir George allow this inspection?"

"My wife thinks so, they went off together. Lord Frederic's body was lying in the Poor House Mortuary to await the Coroner's Inquest. She could hear no more," he finished regretfully.

"You are a natural spy, Scroggs."

"Yes, sir, thank you, sir." He added:

"Dr Seaton is all about the town, sir, on account of the new infection. Many have it. It is in my house."

When Jack Scroggs had departed, the Major said: "I saw your face when he spoke of Dr Seaton."

"I do not like that man," said Denny with force. "He makes my flesh creep."

"He has a little reputation in the town, but I have never been able to get to the bottom of it. He looks so respectable; a professional man, but..." Mearns paused. "It is on a par with wanting to examine Lord Frederic's organs... they say he likes to take a look."

Denny ground his teeth, thinking of Miss Burney. "I think we ought to look at Dr Seaton."

But Dr Seaton, although said to be on the town, treating patients in the increasing sickness, was hard to find. He had been here, they said in one house, but was now gone, and suggested an address in the next street, where they said, Yes, they had seen him, but the patient had died, and he had moved on.

Crying, they said, poor honest fellow.

Which was not what Sergeant Denny thought him.

Fanny came back into the room where Mindy was waiting for her.

"Is there any news of the King?"

Fanny shook her head. "No, the Queen knows nothing. Poor Queen, to have a mad husband."

"And a violent one too."

"She is very distressed, the worry about the children in the nursery and the new spotted illness... I gave the Queen some camphor julep... she was so cold, her hand like marble on mine, the cold went to my heart's core."

Mindy shook her head. "You should not let her distress affect you yourself, miss."

Fanny sighed. "Mr Goldworthy came in just as I was leaving. He was complaining that he had been fagging away and now coming in like a drowned rat, with not a dry thread about him. The Queen offered him some barley water." Fanny laughed.

"Not what he wanted."

"No, indeed... He thinks the King is leading them on a hunt on purpose, that he was laughing at them all the time," she sighed. "Or even that he is hiding somewhere secret and laughing at them as they run around in the wet and cold."

"Could that be so?" Mindy liked the notion, a good joke, she thought.

"The Queen does not think so, but then she does not wish to think evil of the King. Or she doesn't want him laughed at." Perhaps for her they were the same thing, It was hard to know what the Queen thought of King George: she had been married so young, with no choice. To marry the King of England was a great thing in itself. But then childbirth after childbirth, this had really been the substance of her marriage. The children themselves, all the princesses and the royal dukes were perhaps no great joy to her. "But the King does like what he calls 'a good joke.'" She could imagine the King laughing.

His Majesty was hiding, and he was laughing. He had very few opportunities for real mirth in Court Life, other than those he made.

His voice was hoarse and rough. Too much laughter, too much shouting.

"I will not go to Kew," he said loudly to the walls of

the small hovel used by the gardeners in which he had secreted himself. "I have an extreme aversion to Kew as my wife knows. She takes me there because she hates me." Sometimes, King George thought the Queen hated him and on other days he hated her.

They had been together too long and never from choice. He had married out of duty. Four sons and how many daughters? He had lost count.

If he went back, he would burst into the most fierce delirium and the Queen would weep and the Princesses moan. Did he know all this or did he invent it?

The laughter left His Majesty and he decided to move on. The streets of Windsor called him. He imagined himself running through the streets, the wind in his hair. Also, he knew a house to go to where he was always welcome.

He was deeply suspicious of all around him, he knew that they lied to him.

Whom did he trust? Who could he run to? His secret house? No, not today.

Not the Queen, not his sons, not his doctors. All told him untruths.

He trusted little Miss Burney. Yes, he could run to her, nestle next to her. If he knew where she was to be found. He paused in his running, trying to remember where he had last seen her. He believed it was last week at the theatre. Pretty Miss Fanny, he would have to be calm and not frighten her. He had left a bloody mark outside where she slept (in itself a most interesting thought) as a loving sign. A deep chuckle rose up inside him. He was the King, after all.

He might have to chase her.

He enjoyed chasing Miss Burney.

It would be enjoyable to see her run and to feel himself running after her. He did not want to frighten her.

Not really frighten he told himself. Scare. Ladies should be scared on occasion.

Outside it was dark night, which suited His Majesty. He knew it was hard to hide if you were the King.

ELEVEN

The Queen, her relations with the King strained that evening, had retired early to her rooms with two of her daughters. When she was angry with His Majesty, her German accent became ever stronger so that even her daughters found her hard to comprehend. Where the King was this little family group did not know, presuming him to be with his gentlemen.

The whole Court was now nervous about the spreading sickness, it was proposed that they move to Kew. Among some courtiers there was the feeling that the illness was preferable to Kew where King, Queen and the Royal family lived closely together with the Court.

But tonight, before retiring with the Princesses, the Queen had declared for Kew. "I have a headache, mamma," the Princess Amelia was heard saying as she followed her mother, and receiving the guttural, growled reply that she would be dosed.

No one wanted Fanny. Miss Burney was free to do what she had always planned to do that evening: go out into the town, with Mindy if Mindy would come, and take medicines and help to a family which was sick.

Mindy was critical. "I have been poor, miss, and been offered what is called charity and it gives more comfort to the giver than to those that get it."

"Mindy," cried Fanny. "You cannot think I mean harm."

"No, Miss Burney, I never think that of you, but poor people have their pride."

Fanny got up from the sofa where she had been sitting to pace the room. Mindy, who was folding clothes ready to take them to the wash, stood still, watching her mistress. Fanny was always elegant even when tired. Now she wore a plain blue skirt and a matching silk jacket with a show of muslin at wrist and throat.

Fine clothes to go nursing in, thought Mindy, who knew she would be responsible for the laundering of the muslin. But ladies never thought of such toil.

Irritated, she spoke more sharply than she usually allowed herself to speak to her mistress.

"And who is this family of which you feel so much concern?" Fanny was silent. Then: "Tansy Gomer's children."

"Ah."

"Her again."

In London, at the Orange Coffee House, there was a serving woman called Mrs Gomer, she had got a place for a daughter, Tansy, in Dr Burney's house in St Martin's Street in Leicester Fields.

Tansy had helped in the nurseries where Fanny was just growing up. Tansy so pretty and bright had been easy for a child to love, and Fanny had loved her.

But Tansy had been seduced by an actor from Drury Lane and become with child, she had been dismissed without a character. Fanny was supposed to know nothing of this sad history but, of course, she did know.

Tansy had disappeared. Or apparently. But Mindy knew that she had kept in touch with Fanny. Mindy herself had come into the Burney family after the sad history of Tansy had been played out. She did not know the girl, had never seen her, but had been told about her both by the kitchen staff and by Fanny. The picture which the parties painted of Tansy was different: the household thought her a trollop while Fanny remembered the kind nursemaid and called her a friend.

Mindy who had dragged herself out of the slums and meant to stay out, and rising higher, because she now saw the way forward, had no sympathy with Tansy. Stupid girl, was her judgement. If you did feel it necessary to part with your maidenhead (and Mindy would be ready to admit that there might be circumstances it was best allowed) then you should take pains to see there was means ready to prevent consequences or to get rid of any at once if these failed. It could be done, and in her view, should be done.

Naturally, she did not express these views to Fanny. For ladies saw things in a different way. Or anyway, pretended to do so, for Mindy knew as a fact that great ladies had their own ways of dealing with birth and its prevention.

"So she's in Windsor. How did you know?"

"I had a message, a note, she can write... a little... you know."

"And how did she know where to find you?"

"Everyone in my father's house knows, she could find out there."

And you are a published author, thought Mindy. Famous. Gossiped out. Yes, Tansy would want to hang on to you, miss.

"And where does she live?"

"The address was Addeys Close... it's at the bottom of the hill by the river."

"Not a very nice place to live," said Mindy grimly, she had passed the place. A narrow passage with houses leaning forward on each other on either side of the road which was an open drain, one degree lower than Bells Yard in social comforts. She looked at her mistress with a question in her eyes. The relationship between them was changing as she asked her questions, so that it was as if she was Fanny's equal, but she must not push this too far.

"No, I have not been there yet, Mindy," Fanny spoke with dignity. "I want you to come with me."

That's a real lady for you, thought Mindy with respect. She knows her manners.

"They are sick," went on Fanny, "So I must take medicine as well as food."

Thinking that money would be what Tansy was after, Mindy said that she would ask for some soup in the kitchen, there was always food there, often going to waste, they ate well, did the King's servants.

Addey's Close was as unpleasant as Mindy remembered it. Addey had been a master felt maker, and as well as his name he had left behind a ghost of the nauseous stink that went with felt making. Addey, son and grandson, were long since dead and gone, but their name remained on the alley where the long low building where the felting had gone on was now divided into tenements.

Fanny and Mindy paused at the mouth of the Close. It was a very dark narrow entry, noisome and unhealthful. Fanny had not thought to find such a place in Windsor, but Mindy's silence was unsurprised. There was now a newly risen moon so they could see what lay ahead and hear too. They could hear voices, children calling, babies crying, dogs barking and snarling, surely there was a fight going on, and certainly two cats screaming.

For a moment it was dark as the moon went behind a cloud, and then they saw children playing, and women leaning against the wall of the Close, talking to each other while their men folk stood smoking.

A silence fell at the head of the Close as they saw the two visitors and gradually spread down it. The two young women hesitated, then drew close together and entered the Close.

"Mind where you walk," said Mindy, keeping her feet out of the stream of excrement, urine and dirty water that ran down the middle of the Close. "Do you see Tansy here?"

"No. I'm looking. She said she lived at the end of the Close."

Fanny walked forward a few paces when she was stopped by a woman coming out of the darkness. "Burney? You Dr Burney's daughter?"

Fanny said she was.

A man leaning against the wall called out: "The gal you want is up the stairs at the end. She can't come out, she's sick, or the weans are."

The woman who had spoken muttered that she wouldn't go in, not her, she wouldn't.

"Mind your tongue, Bell," growled the man. "You be ill yourself one day."

Fanny and Mindy made their way down the alley. "How many children does she have now?" wondered Fanny aloud. And whose children were they, but this she did not say aloud.

"One for every year since you last saw her," muttered Mindy. "But most will already be dead."

Fanny kept silent as they came to the last door on her left. A narrow entrance with a door on one side and a broken wooden staircase winding up to another floor.

"Up the stairs," said Mindy gloomily. "Bound to be, she has no money."

"We don't know that."

Mindy did not bother to answer. For her the signs were clear. All were poor who lived in the Close but the

201

poorest lived up the stairs, the poorest of all in the attics just under the roof. It was the way of life.

Tansy was in the attics. They found her because the moon was shining through the broken roof.

She was on the floor, leaning against the wall, a dirty blanket making a kind of bed, another smaller blanket wrapped round her. One child, eyes closed, lying beside while she held another in her arms. Her hair was loose and wild, her dress unkempt.

"Miss Burney, you are come." Her voice was sweeter than Mindy had expected, the accent from the country, it was not a London voice.

"Oh Tansy," said Fanny softly.

Tansy tried to stand up, but Fanny knelt on the floor and held her back. "No, no Tansy, you are too weak."

"We are not always so... so untidy," Tansy started to say. "But the babies have the pink spot."

"And you," said Fanny, looking her in the face. "And you are ill too."

The moon went behind a cloud so that all was dark. Mindy busied herself unpacking the basket, all the while muttering to herself.

Dirty, you can smell the babies, no water up here. Not to see anyway, but who can see? There might be a sink on the landing.

The moon came out and she could see a little. Some clothes hanging up on nails. No bed, but a broken chair or two. No sign of a man anywhere.

Mindy spread out a sheet of cloth which she had taken from the Castle kitchens and spread out the food: bread, butter, cheese, some milk. Little enough.

She looked around her, she had a paper twist of tea leaves which she would turn into a drink if she could find both water and a fire to make it on. She had observed two broken cups.

Tansy saw her. "Downstairs," she said hoarsely, "Bella, she is kind, she keeps a fire alight and will make some tea."

Mindy made her way down the stairs, leaving Fanny cleaning Tansy's face and hands with lavender water. The woman Bella received her without speaking, holding her hand out for the tea, and putting some aside for herself without asking. Mindy nodded her acceptance, she would have done the same herself.

When she came back upstairs, carrying a tin of hot tea, the attic smelt better and seemed, somehow tidier, as did Tansy herself.

Ah well, she thought, that is lady's work: to tidy up and bring a nice smell.

Fanny had turned her attentions to the child that Tansy held, she looked away and her eyes met Mindy's. The child is dying, her look said.

"Drink this, Tansy," she said, handing the woman a cup of tea, hot but milky. "Then you must try to eat something."

In the moonlight, it could be seen that a reddish flush covered Tansy's cheeks and spread down her neck.

It is the scarlet fever, Mindy said to herself. I have seen it before. She might even have had herself, in her childhood she had succumbed and recovered from almost every infection that life could offer.

"And both your babies."

"I can't make them drink."

"Come, Tansy, they must drink and so must you," she did not say Or they will die, but Tansy understood.

She whispered: "They are dying. I have seen it before. I know how it comes. They will die whatever is done. I always lose my babies, they die."

Mindy and Fanny looked at each other but found no words to say. Fanny held the cup to Tansy's lips.

"Drink." Tansy drank. "Thank you for coming, Miss Burney," she said as she finished. Her eyes were heavy but her voice sounded stronger. "Thank you."

"Of course. You were right to write to me. I don't forget my friends."

Tansy smiled. Then she said: "But you should not come out in the dark... He is mad."

"Who is?" asked Fanny.

Tansy looked at her, eyes full of fear. "The man who does the killing."

Mindy frowned. "What do you know about this man?"

"I have seen him." Tansy leaned against the wall, closing her eyes. "He tried to kill me. He said I was a trollop and must die."

"Well, you are still here," said Mindy bluntly. "So how?"

"He saw my spots," said Tansy. "And he feared me."

"More than you feared him!"

"Oh, no," said Tansy simply. "I feared him greatly, but he could run and I could not," she sat up and the blanket which covered her fell away.

For the first time, they saw she was heavily with child. Fanny reached out to tuck the blanket around her again. "Oh Tansy," she said, nothing more.

Fanny promised another visit, left some money, and the two walked back down the dark streets back to the Castle.

"The children won't live," said Mindy bluntly.

"She knows it."

"And there is the new one coming soon. Within the month I would say. Probably won't live either. No mention of the father, either. If she knows."

"I fear she may not," said Fanny sadly. "There was no sign of a man living in that place."

They walked on in silence. Mindy aware that her own

fate could have been the same as Tansy, except she had been luckier and cleverer and more determined to rise in the world. Still, there but for the grace of God, she thought.

"And then there is her story," said Fanny. "Did you believe she saw the killer?"

Mindy nodded, she believed. "We must tell the Major and Sergeant Denny."

They walked on in darkness, the moon having gone behind a cloud. Then the clouds parted and in the distance, where the roads divided, they saw a cloaked, tall but hunched figure, carrying a bag and plodding along. All in black like some strange animal.

Both women recognised him. "There goes Dr Seaton," said Fanny. "I knew he went about tending the sick in this illness."

Dr Seaton disappeared into a house, the door banged behind him. It seemed he had been welcomed.

"I shall ask him to call on Tansy," said Fanny. She looked at Mindy who returned an expressionless smile.

If you trust him enough, she was thinking.

"I know he is a strange man in many ways," said Fanny, choosing her words with care. "But he is a man of science, a good doctor, and anxious to help in this sickness. I believe he would help Tansy."

Mindy nodded, still keeping quiet, her thoughts were that being out on the streets at all hours might be one of his pleasures, she had known other men like that, and each had looked for a good excuse. What better than a rampant infection?

"But if it is any comfort to you," went on Fanny, "I will not let him enter my life again," she added: "You must not worry about me, I have had this red sickness. Better if Tansy had had it in the nursery with us," she held out her hand to Mindy. "We must have charity."

I shall teach her the ways of the wicked world if I stay long enough, thought Mindy.

Fanny and Mindy were observed entering the Castle by Major Mearns and Sergeant Denny.

"They should not be out on the town on their own," said the Major whose ideal of female rectitude stayed at home except when taken out by a close male relation. Otherwise they should stay home and keep the house. Children too if they were lucky enough to have any.

"I watch out for them," said Denny. "As much as I can."

"You can't always be on the watch."

"They know the danger, but they think they are safer when together. The streets are lonely, the sickness keeps people at home, but there are the usual oddities about, cloaked, almost masked, hard to identify. One, is certainly Dr Seaton, but there may be another."

"Any name?"

"No name." The Sergeant added in a careful quiet voice: "I hear that the King gets out on occasion. Not for long, and they always get him back. But he has his time of freedom."

Major Mearns sat for a moment in thought. He knew his duties and where his responsibilities lay. "We must tell He who sent us here."

He stood up. "And gather in what information you can about this odd figure."

Denny stood up, too, knocking out the ash from his pipe. "I've seen this person myself. The height and figure of Dr Seaton. Walks like the King."

Was there one strange figure on the streets of Windsor, or two?

THIRTEEN

T he theatre was dark but soon candles and flambeaux would be lighted.

Outside a King might be on the roam, but inside it was work. A new play was preparing in which Winter Ames had the leading part. James Manston was the writer of *The Bride Of Loveden*, a dramatic comedy. He had borrowed the plot from a French original, altered it to suit his cast and thought it should do well. Mr Hills although the manager left much to Manston out of his usual laziness.

A pretty young London actress, Miss Susannah Townely, had been brought down to act with Winter Ames.

"She has performed with Sheridan," said Manston, "and he thinks well of her. She's full young, of course."

"Certainly a lovely face." A full length portrait of Miss Townely had been hung in the entrance of the theatre to encourage an audience.

"Sheridan was in love with her for a while, I believe, I am told she was his mistress for six months, but there is always gossip. And of course, young actresses are apt to have fantasies about famous actors as well having tender hearts." And he looked speculatively at Winter.

Winter did not react. He had no intention of entangling himself with a young actress, especially one who had enjoyed a loving friendship with David Garrick: she was clearly a young woman of ambition as well ability.

"She will be a good actress one day, perhaps even a great once," went on Manston. "But for this play you will have to carry her. She will be popular with the audience, of course. And Mr Sheridan has promised to come down to see her perform."

"Will he brave the current infection?" Many were not doing so, the town was emptying.

"We must behave as if nothing is happening. There are enough tales roaring round the town as it is." Manston sounded glum. "Poor Lord Frederic. A friend, you know, to me and to the theatre."

"Did you know his habits?"

Manston paused. "We all knew or guessed a few, I suppose." He was evasive.

"Sir George has told me that he was dressed like a very poor woman," Winter paused, then added sadly: "Like a woman of the streets. Not the first to die dressed so."

Manston shook his head. "He ought to have worn satin and stiff silks, not torn cottons and second hand rags."

"He wanted to attract the rough sort." As, by God, he did, poor fellow.

Once again Manston fell silent, then he said: "Sir George also said that his body was covered in a rash and it was creeping up his neck." He rubbed his hands together, and looked at his wrists. "He had the new spot. So he might have died anyway."

"Not like that, though."

Manston continued to rub his hands.

"How are you?" Winter asked, wondering if his friend had the pink spot himself. There was an itchy, fidgety look to him.

"Well. Actors are never ill. They may die but they are never sick. Can't afford it."

"Does Miss Townely feel immortal too?"

Manston smiled. "Oh yes, an actress appearing in her

first important leading part is never unwell."

"Die first, eh? Like you?"

"Something of the sort."

"I don't think I'm for dying," said Winter Ames. For that matter, nor did he think Manston was either. He kept an open mind about ambitious young actresses.

They were standing on the stage which had a steep rake. Manston looked around him. "We can use the same curtains and furniture that we used for *The Lost Bride*. The costumes too, Miss Townely is slight and not over tall. Wigs also will fit. They can always be padded underneath if too big."

He looked appraisingly at Winter Ames. "Your costumes should fit but we can get small alterations if necessary. In the first act, when you are a poor wanderer, or pretending to be so, it won't matter if they are loose..." He gave Winter another sharp look, "You are much less stout than Jerome Edwards who wore them last..."

—And I am cleaner and I do not smoke so much, I hope someone has aired the clothes since Jerome wore them, thought Winter, but he did not say so aloud. Sharing the costumes was something all actors got used to. Fleas too, he hoped someone had got rid of the fleas. Fleas were a hard cross to bear, especially someone else's fleas.

Providing your own clothes was another problem which could be a severe drain on a poor actor, although it was possible to hire them in Monmouth Street in London. As well not to hire yourself clothes that put your leading actor and manager in the shade or you stood a chance of losing your part. Such happened to an actor who hired a better coat than David Garrick and was relieved of his part in consequence. Most actors were poor. Winter Ames was a little richer than most because of some family money.

"How many rehearsals?" Winter asked, knowing Hills liking for little in that line. Money again. Never enough in the theatre, not even if you are a Garrick or a Sheridan.

Manston frowned. "Three. One with the book."

The theatre in Windsor was under Royal Patronage and exceedingly respectable but even the Theatre Royal had its disorderly customers.

"Is anyone back stage?" asked Winter.

Manston shook his head. "No, the place is empty. We are alone."

"I thought I heard someone."

They both listened. "A door banging, I thought." Or someone falling, the sound was very little different.

"The wind," said Manston, and it was true that the wind blew through all the cracks and crevices in the old theatre. None of the doors fitted. "There are always noises here, haven't you noticed?"

Winter had heard, he was well used to theatre noises, but somehow these noises sounded different.

Windsor felt different these days, as did the theatre. Infection, murder and blood.

Blood in the castle itself. Mindy had told him that blood had come close to Fanny Burney. All the murder victims were women.

Or, in the case of Lord Frederic, had dressed as a woman. Poor Lord Fred.

"Do you think it would be a good idea to talk to Major Mearns about the murders?" he asked Manston.

"What does he know?"

"He might know more than we do."

"That would not be difficult," said Manston.

"Quelle horreur," murmured Winter.

Manston looked at him sharply: "What's that?"

"Just a line from a play I acted in once."

"I never know when to believe you, Winter, or not. I think you Yankees see things differently from the subjects of the King."

"We were subjects of King George until very recently. My family in Philadelphia are surprised that they are so no longer."

"It will be best not to speak too much of that in Windsor. Talk of the American Rebellion is not popular, especially now when we see what is happening in France."

"There is blood on the streets of Windsor now," said Winter Ames, his face expressionless.

"I do not understand you there." Manston shook his head. "Here we have no rioting citizens, no starving peasantry. I don't think anyone who knows Windsor could think that likely to happen… That is, I believe there was a little rising a time ago in one of the barracks, but it was soon put down without too much hanging."

Just a hanging or two, thought Winter Ames, nothing to signify.

Manston hurried off, muttering to himself that no one must be late.

Ames watched him go, his thoughts full. Here I am, in this country which is not foreign but which is strange to me in so many ways. In this country, I suspect I have fallen in love. But with which woman: Miss Burney or Mindy?

Thank God, I have faced that double fact. At home, in Philadelphia we have had a revolution. Here in England, the King is mad, the Queen wishes him to retire and her son to rule in his place (except no one rules in England without the Parliament's permission) and in Windsor an infection rages and a murderer stalks.

This is a gothic tale, by God.

Horace Walpole himself could not do better.

Still, he must prepare himself for the evening's performance. There was a moon, all the links were lit on the road to the theatre, so there would be a full house.

Or there would be if enough people would brave the pink, spotted sickness which was not measles but something nastier. Miss Townely arrived early still carrying the text, and enquiring anxiously if the prompter was efficient.

"Does the King keep thumbscrews in his Theatre Royal, Windsor?" she asked Winter Ames, shedding her mantle while adjusting her fashionably flowing hair.

"I don't think so. I think they went out of use a few decades ago. Why?"

She sighed. "Because soon he will discover that I do not know my lines," she gave Winter a flirtatious smile. Her London manager had already sent the message down from London: Watch Miss Townely. Give Susy half a finger hold and you will be lost. Seduction is her game. Trust me, I know.

It was sometimes difficult to be sure when Mr Sheridan was joking but on this occasion, Winter Ames felt sure he was not.

She was a beauty though, with her deep, dark eyes and pale skin, but fortunately not one to Winter's taste.

Manston did not seem attracted either. But you could never tell with Jem Manston. A enigma with a smile.

The smile could fade sharply, as Winter knew well, if the receipts from the last production were not as high as he had expected, or if an actor (even more an actress) failed to attract the audience. Actresses, Manston believed, were there to bring in the passing trade and hold on to those with annual tickets. Actors kept the plot of the play going as heroes, villains or comics.

Since Winter was here to learn the ways of the English theatre and to find some new plays to take back to America, he behaved politely to his colleague and did not let him see that he thought him a bully.

"They are his own lines too. I understand he wrote the play."

"In a way," agreed Winter cautiously. He did not think that anyone had written this play they were to perform soon. It had been put together, with lines copied from here and there. No doubt he might find a bit of *Macbeth* in it if he listened hard. To be sure, many other authors had contributed without knowing it.

Then he remembered how unlucky it was to call up the name of the Scottish play and wondered if it was equally unlucky to even let the name cross the mind.

He looked at Miss Townely and hoped she would survive: they had lost one leading actress already.

"I suppose the lines will be pinned up all over so that I can read my cues... that is all that really matters, is it not, because I can make what I have to say."

She saw a look of doubt on Winter Ames' face as he thought that, although they might not be very good lines, they were the lines laid down by James Manston who was apt to be possessive about what he had decreed.

"It is of no consequence, after all, as long as I move the action of the play along in the right direction." And she gave a merry laugh. "There is not usually much variety in these matters: Lovers meet, lovers embrace, undying devotion, lovers quarrel, he thinks she is false (or the other way round, you know), the hero is sent to prison, or she is kidnapped, sometimes both, lovers make up. Play ends."

"There might be a little violence in this play," Winter had read the whole play through and knew that vile things were offered to the heroine, although tactfully masked when on stage so no sensibilities would be offended.

But those who wished to imagine could.

Susannah shrugged. "Oh I am accustomed to rapine and murder twice a night when performing," she offered him a winning smile, which, he was beginning to perceive, meant nothing at all. "I will win through, you will see, my dear American."

She lowered her voice: "Mr Sheridan assured me that I would have no trouble with Mr Manston."

He knew what she meant: some actor managers thought the body of a young actress was one of the perquisites of the job. Manston wasn't one to behave like that in Winter's view. Not at all.

"No, you won't," he agreed.

"Mr Sheridan laughed as he said it."

"Did he?"

"He praised his style."

Susannah studied Winter's face, seeming satisfied with what she read there, she went on: "Not much sense of humour, though."

"Did Mr Sheridan say that also?"

She did not answer. Across the room, the figure of Manston was advancing. With a frown, she said: "I must ask him about my costumes and if they are fresh."

Winter Ames knew they were not. They were old and used more than once, like the dialogue of the play.

There was a short rehearsal, the entrances and exits only, no time for more as Manston pointed out, during which Miss Townely refused to wear the clothes supplied, claiming they smelt, which could not be denied. With an angry face, that aged her and made her look shrewish, she wore her own.

Under her breath she hissed that there would be a bill to pay on this account. Those of the cast who heard her, and Winter Ames was one, knew she would have some task to get the money out of James Manston.

The House was not crowded since the pink fever kept many at home, and those who were not sick, thought it wiser to stay away from crowds. In fact, the House was papered, which the experience cast recognised. It did not improve their performance which further angered the new recruit who swore quietly under her breath as she moved round the stage. Nor was the temper of Manston improved.

Since he was not in the middle act of the play, a five

acter, all were pleased when his glowering face disappeared.

"Gone for a drink," said the prompter, who also understudied all male members of the cast which meant that sometimes he was running round the stage with the prompt book. "God help us." For Manston was not a drinker and drinking did not improve his mood.

The play was not being well received, the laughs were not coming, nor the sudden chilling silence when the heroine, Clara, was confronted with the Monster in the Closet.

The Monster had no words to say in this scene which was just as well since the prompter was taking the part and he could not read the lines through his mask.

It was to be hoped that Susannah did not need prompting, but she was proving adept at inventing what she had to say. Usually, she allowed herself a good scream and then much anxious breathing, this, as she had learnt in Drury Lane, could see her through many a moment. "Learn how to pant, my dear," an early instructor in the art of deceiving audiences, had said. "Charmingly, of course, not as if you had been running. Pant with love, with fear, with happiness, and panting will stand you in good stead."

Winter Ames, obliged to stand close, found the panting unpleasant. Miss Townely had been eating onions.

He was glad that his own last meal had been quiet and frugal: a sort of gruel, it had tasted of nothing, his landlady in Peascod Street, being a sad cook.

Miss Townely did not withdraw her lips, instead, they pressed closer.

Not much reaction from the audience, for which he really could not blame them. When the house is largely papered, then there has to be something of a sensational nature on stage to get much of a reaction.

He knew that he and Susannah were not sensational.

"Dear Love," she said. And that was not in the script, he

thought, for he knew it better than she did.

She kissed him again, he stumbled backward.

From the audience, hitherto quiet if not somnolent, there came a laugh.

One laugh, then a high scream, a scream of terror. And another.

Then silence.

On stage, Winter Ames stopped in the middle of his ardent protestation of love. Susannah gripped his arm.

"Is a revolution?"

"No, of course not." For all I know, it could be, thought Winter, except that is not how we did it in my country. This might be the European way.

There was no more screaming but both performers were conscious of movement and voices coming from the gallery.

They finished their scene well aware that the best attention of the audience was not on them. Winter noticed a perceptible movement in the audience with couples getting up. After the interval they would be lucky to have an audience at all.

When they came off, Winter demanded to know what was going on.

Susannah fluttered after him: "What was it? Pray tell."

James Manston came from the wings and told them bluntly that a woman in the audience saw a masked figure prowling in the empty seats behind her.

"Thought she was going to be attacked, so she screamed."

"Yes, we heard."

"Everyone did. I rushed up there. So did the stage manager, so did your understudy. No one there."

"All her imagination?"

Manston shrugged.

"She was very upset," said the stage manager, suddenly

appearing and speaking up. "Very upset. I think she saw something."

"Saw something?" Winter Ames disliked slovenly talk. "What something? Alive or dead?"

"Oh, alive all right. That was what she didn't like. What frightened her. Didn't look human, all black and hooded, but it moved..." He added: "And that was when she screamed."

"So?" asked Winter. "What did you see?"

"Nothing," said Manston. "I was there first and there was nothing and no one."

The stage manager nodded his agreement.

"So she imagined it?"

"Nearly emptied the house," said James Manston, "did you notice them getting up and shuffling out?"

Nearly all paper anyway, thought Winter Ames.

"Not all imagination though," said the stage manager. From the deep pocket of his linsey overall he dragged a knife.

A strange knife, with a serrated edge. There was blood on it. Old dried blood.

"Do you think he is a knacker, or a butcher?"

Susannah gave a little scream. "That is not a butcher's knife."

"No," said Winter, looking at it. "Nor a cook's. No kitchen knife, that."

"A surgeon," said Susannah. "My brother in law is a surgeon, he has such a knife. Thank goodness the blood is dried and not fresh."

"There was fresh blood," said James Manston. "A streak of it on the wall and one of the seats up there."

Ames frowned: "If he did not injure the woman, which I thank God he did not, and the blood on this knife is dried, then he must have brought the blood with him."

The stage manager spoke, moving his hands nervously:

"I think he likes blood."

Winter Ames marched forward. "I am going to look at the blood."

James Manston clapped his hands together. "The performance! The play must go on."

"If there is any audience left to watch," said Winter over his shoulder.

Susannah, who had been quiet, urged him not to get blood on him.

"There wasn't so much," said the stage manager, "but it was wet." He followed Winter to show him where it was.

"What happened to the woman who screamed?"

"She ran off, down the stairs and away. Couldn't blame her. There weren't more than a dozen people up here in the gallery." He looked around. All the seats were empty. "And they've gone too. Can't blame them."

He pointed out the bloody stains on the back of the seat, three rows back, and on the floor. "Drying already. Well, I suppose it wasn't very fresh blood, after all he had to bring it with him."

Winter studied the blood which had made three separate stains: a big spreading circle on the floor as if a jug of blood had poured down, a smaller stain on the first seat in the aisle, as if a hand had dragged itself along making marks with its fingers, and a tiny stain on the back.

"What did the woman say?"

"Not much, she was already running down the stairs, she just said a weird man."

"Did she say if he touched her or threatened her?"

"Nothing like that but she did say his face was hidden and he was in black. A big man. But she was a small woman."

"But you didn't see him?"

The man shook his head. He seemed relieved rather than disappointed.

James Manston's voice calling from below recalled Winter Ames to the stage where the curtains were about to part. When Winter Ames and Susannah saw the ragged rows of their audience with many empty seats, only the sheer professionalism of both kept them on the stage.

For the first time, Winter admired his lovely colleague as she gritted her teeth, almost visibly, and went on with the dialogue.

"Dear love, I am terrified."

Winter folded her in his manly arms, and murmured: "And so is what is left of the audience."

FOURTEEN

The only remaining magistrate in Windsor at that time was Sir Joseph Daly, the rest had fled the infection. Mr Pitt had had his secretary get in touch with him when the communication from Major Mearns had reached him. There was no doubt that the death of the Lord Frederic Bertie, the dousing of the theatre with blood, the rumours of the King's behaviour interested and alarmed Mr Pitt.

"You must tell Daly that this matter in Windsor must be dealt with. I know Joe Daly, he will do as he is told. Windsor, of all places, there should be no murders and sickness in Windsor. We cannot have the King endangered."

"No, sir," Mr Pitt's secretary had said.

"And even more, we cannot have the King roaming killing innocent citizenry. We have enough trouble with the Prince of Wales, but seduction is his game, not murder."

Mr Pitt laughed and his secretary dutifully followed but there was no mirth in the sound.

"Tell Sir Joseph to give the Major all the assistance he needs... Short of arresting the King..." Another laugh. "In public."

Sir Joseph was always delighted to be in touch with Mr Pitt even at third hand, for the private secretary had written the letter and yet another more insignificant person had delivered it. By hand.

A matter of such importance, so confidential in its message and subject matter, could not be entrusted to any postal system.

Sir Joseph took it from the hand of the messenger himself and broke the seal while offering the man who had brought it some refreshment while he indited a reply.

The messenger, by name Lamb, was pleased to wait and take some wine and cold beef. He knew from an earlier visit that Sir Joe looked after you well, whereas in the Castle the King would offer you some cold barley water. If you got down to the kitchens it was another matter, of course, food and drink in abundance. Nothing stinted, all of first class quality, they lived well in the kitchens, better there than at the royal table probably.

Lamb would like to have looked in on a lady he knew who lived in Peascod Lane and in whose company he had some entertainment, but alas, he knew he must ride back to London tonight with Sir Joseph's reply. He was deemed too unimportant to know what was in the letter, which same unimportance meant that Mr Pitt and his secretary discussed matters freely in front of him as if he had no ears.

Socially speaking, he supposed he had not.

As it was, he knew that the King was suspected of a ghastly series of deaths, but that he was mad so no one need blame him nor even know. He could be sent into a quiet retreat and the Prince of Wales would act in his place.

Lamb drank his wine while he waited. Perhaps it was just as well that he could not visit Mrs Dorothy Benet in her welcoming house because he had heard there was a new pox going about Windsor from which people were dying.

Sir Joseph came back into the room, holding out a folded and sealed sheet. "Take this to Mr Pitt."

When Lamb had ridden away, Sir Joseph sent a message to Major Mearns requesting that he call at Camden House which was the new house which Sir Joseph had caused to be built on the Datchet Road.

"It will be the business in the theatre that has caused this alarm." The Major had heard early that morning about the screams and the blood in the theatre last night, from Winter Ames himself who knew something, if not all, of what the Major was, and thought he should know. Winter always had Fanny and Mindy on his mind. "Stories are getting about."

"Like the King," observed Denny sardonically. He had not got far in his search for the identity of the strange figure seen in Windsor and suspected of the killings. "I went to the theatre to inspect the blood, it was dry by then, but had not been long dry. No body to be found."

"You saw Winter Ames?"

"He showed me where to look. Mr Manston was otherwise engaged."

"He often is, I fancy," said Mearns thoughtfully. "What did you make of Ames?"

"He is a clever man."

"So he is, we play whist together in the Gentlemen's Club. He plays a good hand."

"He is as puzzled by blood as I was. He is puzzled by the whole affair, I think."

"So where did the blood come from?"

Denny shrugged. "From a dead cat, a shot dog, or a butcher's or a knacker's yard. I shall find out."

"Or a body that has not been found?"

"Blood does not flow freely from the dead, only the living, you and I have been on the battlefield, sir, and know it. And there was much blood. This blood must have been brought to the theatre in a jug or a jar or a bucket."

"That is a very interesting thought, Denny."

The two men eyed each other. "But not one to pass on to Sir Joseph."

The Major and of course, Sergeant Denny, knew more about Sir Joseph than the knight knew of them.

Denny summed it up for them both: "Rich, made his own money out in India, married to a very beautiful wife whom he met in India, the widow of a soldier. No children, lives a quiet life in Windsor but in London, where he goes frequently, is a friend of Mr Pitt and Mr Pitt's circle."

The Major too knew Mr Pitt, not as a friend but in a professional way, he knew he was valuable to Pitt.

This view was reinforced by the courtesy with which both men were received at Camden House.

Sir Joseph came down to greet them and took them into his library. On the stairs they passed Lady Daly (who had, in fact, stationed herself there to see them). Her ladyship curtseyed and the two men bowed. She had heard the Major had a great skill as a lover and was anxious to view him. She concluded that, although older than she had expected, the reports did not lie.

The Major noticed her ladyship, but business was business and he passed on, merely observing that here was a game that he might come back to.

Sir Joseph did not mince his words... Don't hold on to things, not how I learnt in India, he said to himself, this is how business is done. Brisk and open.

What he had to say was a surprise to them. "Mr Pitt has learned from his informants."

Spies, Mearns thought, he did not name himself among them for he knew that Mr Pitt had informants other than himself.

"That for several nights the King has been out, missing, and not back until the small hours, Once even later. In disarray, tired, as if he had been excited."

They know a lot, these informants, thought Mearns.

"And was now exhausted. Clothes muddy." sir Joseph added, speaking carefully: "And last night there was blood on his clothes."

Mearns thought for a moment. "Who else knows about this?"

"The Queen does not."

Mearns nodded. "Wise."

"And I am ordered to forget, Major."

What strange ways they have of going on in Courts, thought Mearns. He will not forget, probably it is not even expected he will forget, but if he should talk of it now, then he is a liar. It is how governments work.

But I am ordered to remember. At least for the moment.

They were bowed out, after another offer of wine, which they refused. Lady Daly was not seen as they left, but a twitch of the curtain in the big front window suggested she might be there.

During all this time, Denny had said nothing.

But as they walked through the streets, in step and both without consultation going towards the theatre, he said: "How could the King get in and out without anyone knowing?"

"You forget, he has been King since he was a boy, there are so many ways in and out of that old castle, not all known to the adult world, but a boy would find them out. We know he knows about the door in the privy, there will be others."

"So what is out duty?"

"To find out the truth, Denny, that is always our duty."

Winter Ames was waiting for them in the theatre entrance. He held out his hand. "Welcome." He smiled at Denny: you again the smile said "Manston is not here, was not here when you came, Sergeant, he has had to go to London, he has left me in charge... The truth is he does not want to talk about it, we may look and speculate and even feel afraid but he wants none of it, so he is off the London. I think he blames himself although I have no idea why."

"Guilt does spread itself around," observed the Major, looking around him with keen, bright eyes. Denny stood silently behind him. His part was to he the observer.

"I told the Sergeant all I knew, I was on stage when the man was there and the woman screamed… there was nothing to see except blood."

"The woman?" queried Mearns.

"We now have the name and address of the woman who screamed, Mrs Eleanor Willis. She had a courtesy ticket since she owns a shop in the town, an apothecary's in Sheet Street, and lets the theatre put up play bills." He added by way of explanation: "She was recognised as she ran out."

"You have spoken to her?"

"No, Major, I have left that to you. I do not think she would welcome anyone from the theatre," Winter said dryly. "I fancy she will trust you more."

He was leading them through a corridor to the green room. "This is where we sit when not on stage."

"I know," said Mearns. "I have sat in the greenroom myself on occasion as a guest."

Winter smiled. "Dr Johnson did the same, but found the ladies' white bosoms too inflaming, so Davy Garrick claimed."

"I found the whitelead wash that they cover the flesh with the reverse of inflaming. And the bright blue round the eyes and the red patches on the cheeks."

"It is so the faces will be seen even from the pit," said Winter with apology.

There was a silence as what might be called the polite preliminaries were concluded.

The Major murmured a few sentences about the intervention of Sir Joseph Daly which had brought him here. "I come as servant of the government." He did not mention Mr Pitt, but in his mind that name was never forgotten. -

"Mr Manston had a message from Sir Joe, whom he

knows, and deputed me to show you want." He added sardonically: "Mr Hill still being absent."

"Not show, Sergeant Denny has inspected the bloody stains, he tells me there was plenty of it. Was a bucket left behind?"

Winter shook his head.

"Well, let us see what you could provide," said Mearns easily. "Having been on the battlefield we know the vessels and instruments that can be used for a different purpose."

He led the way through the back corridors of the theatre. "Downstairs first," he said, still easily, "then up next if we find nothing here."

But Winter Ames noticed that the Major kept him engaged in a light conversation, while his eyes ranged everywhere, and while Sergeant Denny occupied himself with opening cupboards and inspecting all dark corners.

It was Denny who found, rather as a hound will find the trail. They heard him give a soft but audible cry. "Here."

He was pointing to a row of buckets, half of which were filled with sand, the others with water.

"It is in case of fire." Winter offered the explanation promptly. "You know the danger of fire in a theatre."

For answer, Denny pointed to a bucket tucked away at the back of the others which was smaller, of a different quality, and empty.

"That stain on the bottom," he said with conviction, "is blood."

Winter bent to stare into the bucket. "All the blood, all brought into the theatre and all spent here?" He sounded aghast, as if it was hard to believe.

"All in and all spent," said Denny softly, with apparent satisfaction.

Mearns gave his sergeant an approving nod. It was the ability to find such evidence when needed that he had chosen Sergeant Denny, He knew this, and probably Denny knew it too. What Mearns did not know was that he himself had been chosen for his sharpness of observation coupled with his knowledge of men and women.

Mearns nodded again, half to himself. "Let us go to speak to the lady who was accosted in the theatre. Mrs Willis in Sheet Street, was it not?"

Mrs Willis lived above the shop which was run by her son, a tall thin young man called Giles. Mrs Willis herself was small, plump and fair skinned with curly hair which was going grey. She was dressed neatly in black with a little white collar.

"I am a widow, sir," she explained. "My husband died two years ago, but Giles is trained, he makes up the medicines, the pills and the lotions. For a while I worked in the castle, but now I help in the shop. We are very busy at the moment, as you may guess, with all the illness. Dr Seaton has called on us a lot."

"It is a bad time," agreed Mearns.

"I do dearly love the theatre so I took the ticket for my seat gladly. Mr Hill and indeed Mr Manston too, are both always as generous with spare tickets as can be, Mr Manston is much admired in the town... You too, sir," she said, giving Winter Ames a little curtsey.

She began to shiver a little. "Oh yes, I saw him, sir. Just a look over my shoulder as I felt... smelt... someone there. A glimpse... A large man, tall, big in every way. All in black, head and face covered in black... He touched my shoulder, I screamed. I ran past him and out."

"He didn't follow you?"

She hesitated. "I believe he came after me, but he was slow, and doing something, throwing something around."

"She does not know about the blood," said Mearns to his companions as they left. "And as for us, we must find

where it came from and who bought this bucket of blood...
It was a business transaction, I think."

"You can buy blood?" asked Winter Ames.

"Oh yes, fresh blood. One would not want it stale."

Winter gave him a wary look, as if he feared there was a
joke on him in this. "What's it used for?"

Mearns thought about it. "Certain dyes perhaps, perhaps
some other crafts might use it, leather work may be, although for them it would not matter if it was old blood.
And for food... sausages, pies, a meat jelly, yes, it is used
in recipes. Hares are jugged in their own blood."

"The knacker's yard down by the Datchet Road is the
biggest and best in the town," said Denny. "I am for going
there and asking questions."

"Do you want to come, Mr Ames?" asked Mearns.

Winter nodded slowly and without pleasure. He thought
he should go with them.

They were greeted at Fleckers by a tall, thick armed
woman, her hair braided on the top of her head. She wore
a thick leather apron over a dark serge skirt.

"Oh yes, sir, I slaughter the animals. I live by killing the
beasts."

"A strange trade for a woman," said Mearns, in a friendly
way, anxious to get the best information he could out of
her. This is a woman's town for sure, he said to himself,
we shall be having a female sovereign next.

"My father was a butcher, I was apprenticed to him, and
I married into this business."

"What's that, Mary?" called a deep voice from the depth
of the killing shed. "What's afoot?" A tall, burly fellow came
out of the shed. "Oh it's you Major," and he rubbed his
hands over his apron to clean them, before holding one
out.

Mearns looked at him. "Corporal Flecker... you served
with me in India."

"No, sir, you are wrong there, I never got further than Chatham to be embarked: my father died and I was bought out."

To the question about the sale of blood, it appeared that there were several regular buyers: a meat pie shop, a sausage maker, and a maker of dyes in Staines.

"He could buy his blood local," explained Flecker, "but he thinks our blood is better... cleaner, sir, we are careful about being clean." He rubbed his hand on his shirt sleeve this side.

Had he had any request for blood yesterday. Or the day before?

He looked at his wife who nodded. Yes, several, all known to them, old customers. John Barley from the Pie Shop, Edward Coomb who made dyes and seemed to need blood for his black dye, and Mrs Charlotte Frame, sausage maker... she sold in the market and went round with a barrow when there was no market. All could be easily found, sir.

"Anyone else?"

It appeared there had been.

Mrs Flecker nodded. "I looked after him, Jim, you was out taking your refreshment." She turned to the three men. "You gets thirsty in this job, so we all drink a bit, and none the worse for it."

"Of course not, Mrs Flecker," said Mearns. "Wouldn't think ill of you for a moment. So who was it? Someone you knew?"

She shook her head. "Jim saw him as he came back in."

Flecker nodded: "A big feller, all in black, big hat pulled down, scarf on his face, didn't want us to see him, some is shy of buying blood." He scratched his head, and his wife spoke: "Talked like a German."

The three men walked away in silence. Then Mearns said: "I cannot think that helps us find the man in black who bought blood in a German accent, but it certainly gives us something to think about." He looked at his companions: "Does it not?"

The King, Windsor Castle and blood seemed bound together in the minds of Mearns and Denny.

But Winter Ames kept his own counsel.

FIFTEEN

Windsor was the city of fever and blood. This expression was not used, it was not talked about in the shops and in the drinking houses or in the polite tea and whist parties of Windsor, but it was how people felt. As professionals in the business, the Major and Denny did not call it such to each other but there was tension and apprehension in the back of each man's mind. Like being in a battle.

Was it a war? And whom were they fighting? In the theatre, Winter Ames and James Manston met to discuss the poor audience figures, which they blamed on the current feeling in the town and to consider closing the production down. Yes, for them it was a war.

The mood was sombre in the Castle because the King was known to be ill and it was suspected he was uncontrollable. Not all the details of the murders in the town were known to the Court, but the death of Lord Frederic Bertie was a painful reality. A reminder, if they needed one, that being close to the King and Queen did not always protect you.

Fanny guessed that disquieting stories, exaggerated rumours no doubt, had reached London and her father, for Dr Burney had written suggesting she give up her good post and come home.

"You find it tiring, exhausting even, my dear daughter, so I advise that you tender your resignation to the Queen."

Fanny folded the letter and put it in her reticule. She wished this letter to be private to her and she knew that any letters left on her writing table or a work basket were read by Mindy as a matter of course. It was a practise tacitly admitted to by both women and not resented by Fanny who saw that it was useful to have Mindy aware of a great deal that was going on in her mistress's life. They were close and confidential with each other, it was the way of life, and if Mindy knew more about Fanny than Fanny knew about her, that was the way of life too. And if Fanny managed a few secrets with the aid of her reticule in which a letter from Winter Ames nestled next to the letter from her father, that was right too.

"Dear Miss Burney," Ames had written. "I am one of those who admire your writing. Miss Burney, as a sincere admirer, may I say that nature did not devise you to be a courtier, you should leave the Castle, return to London and *write*."

There was more in the letter still that Fanny would keep to herself; praising her with vigour. Colonials were allowed to be enthusiastic. She was heartened by his praise.

Winter Ames, as he had written his letter, knew that he had more to say to her than he had dared to write. He could not write to her of the love that a man feels for a woman, and yet he wished he could have dared to do it. What would a woman like Fanny Burney say if she received a letter of passionate love?

And then, had he really got such love to offer? There was Charlotte Minden who also aroused strong feelings. He admired Charlotte too, but in a totally different way from Miss Burney.

Actors were famously fickle.

Could you love two women at once? But then he loved them in such totally different ways: Fanny he loved for her rectitude, her sensitive approach to life, her talent. In short, her mind. Whereas Mindy had a strong physical pull, but he loved her spirit, the way she fought her way through life. What a wife for an impecunious, colonial actor.

No letter to Mindy, but to one of them he must write because he felt that Windsor was dangerous to them both.

Since he had come to England, first joining the Drury Lane company and then coming to take principal parts in Windsor he had come to realise the dual nature of English society. There was the top layer, so sophisticated, gentle mannered and polite, and there was underneath a more savage world that flogged men, sent them to the gallows, used children for whores. A world created out of starvation.

He was now seeing the bloody side of Windsor. There was a killer, a killer of women, and a killer who collected blood in a bucket to daub about the place.

As a joke? Or a warning: I am coming for you next?

Another letter, a note no more, and ill scrawled, was handed to Fanny later that day. She knew it was from Tansy Gomer.

"She is ill, I shall have to go to her. I will go tonight when the Queen sends me away."

But best not to tell Mindy.

The Major and Sergeant Denny were pondering that question too.

"If it is a threat then we ought to warn Mrs Willis because the blood came near her."

"That would mean the killer knew her."

"And knew where to find her... sitting in that seat."

"Or recognised her sitting in that seat."

The Major drew on his pipe. "Pass the pewter pot, Denny."

Denny got up, handed a tankard to the Major which he then filled with ale from a great jug. He took some himself.

"Mrs Hooley has asked us to join her table for dinner tonight," he said as he sat down.

Mrs Hooley was one of the Castle housekeepers, at her table you ate well.

"I accepted. We shall be sure of a good meal."

The Major drew on his pipe, then he said: "We ought to warn Mrs Willis."

Denny nodded. "My thought too. And Miss Burney and Mindy... because there was blood smeared around them. Remember?"

"Oh I remember." The Major stood up. "We should go to all, Denny."

There was a sharp knock on the door and before they could say anything, the door opened and Mrs Hooley came in.

"Gentlemen, you must come to dinner now: the chef has cooked a special French dish that must be eaten when ready, and it is ready now."

As Mearns opened his mouth to request a delay, she put up her hand: "And Mrs Mumby is coming, you cannot be late."

Mrs Mumby was the chief of the Queen's dressers and a person of power and importance in the Castle which even Mearns recognised, and even more how powerful she was in the world in which Mrs Hooley lived and worked.

He looked at Denny, raised an eyebrow and gave a

nod which said: Dinner first, then we go out.

Mrs Hooley swept them along the corridor and up the stairs to her dining room, where they were no longer arrived, than Mrs Mumby came in. It was her habit to make an entrance when all the other guests had arrived, a way she had picked up from her royal mistress. Mearns thought he had caught a glimpse of her bright blue silk skirt round the corner. He and Denny exchanged looks: watching and waiting, it said of Mrs Mumby.

The chef's miracle dish, was a kind of soufflé cum mousse, which did not dent the appetite of two hungry men, but they ate quickly.

Unluckily for them, Mrs Mumby liked to linger over her food, talking, taking the wine, and gossiping.

A large roast of beef followed which was carved at table. Various hot dishes of vegetables were placed around it. The wine was red and good.

"No one who has not served the Queen and the Princesses knows what they are really like. Oh they like a story to laugh at. The Princess Royal is as bad as any of them. Or as good, for I do not count a good laugh as a fault. Only today she said to Miss Burney, for I was a listening—how could I help as I was fastening a brooch upon the Queen's bosom—and the Princess Royal said: "Miss Burney is it really true that, in your illness last year, you coughed so violently that you broke the whalebone of your stays in two?" Miss Burney admitted that it was and her Royal Highness burst into a great peal of laughter."

German laughter, thought the Major.

"Oh my goodness, and then today... the King has gone off no one knows where. Blown away in all the shocking draughts in this castle, I said when I was told."

"And what answer did you get?" asked the Major, draining his wine.

"Oh, that he was often on the loose so that no one knew where he was. I think the Queen begins to mind… Tonight she was quite sharp about it and forbid any talk of it. As if we would, you may rest assured, ma'am, I said, that I would not dream of mentioning that the King goes in and out as he chooses."

The Major looked at Denny who nodded.

"But lor', Mrs Mumby," said their hostess, "he takes his gentlemen with him when he goes."

Mrs Mumby gave a tinkling laugh. "That he doesn't, for they never know he is gone until he is gone. But not sorry they are to miss the outing, for they hate his great walks, fagging away, they call it and glad not to be on it."

As one man, Mearns and Denny, they excused themselves to their hostess, bowed to Mrs Mumby, and nodded to Colonel Goldsbird and Mr Sharp the other guests.

"We won't get asked to dine there again," said Denny, as he hurried after the Major.

"We might if we save the King from great disgrace." Thus the Major over his shoulder as he marched forward to Market Square.

—I don't fancy arresting His Majesty, thought Denny as he hurried on, but if we must, we must.

The sky was darkening, the moon falling behind the clouds which were dropping a soft rain on to the town.

The Market Square lay in the shadow of the castle and the apothecary's shop was on the corner. It was not open for business but a dim light shone from inside.

Mearns advanced, he banged on the door. He listened, then banged again.

"Someone is coming."

Slowly the door was opened by Mr Giles Willis, he was wearing an overall and carrying a candle. "Sir?" he said, in surprise. He blinked as he recognised the Major. "My mother is not here."

"Ah, so where is she?"

"My mother had a ticket sent her for the performance at the theatre to make up to her for what she lost. No," he said quickly, "she is not at the theatre because this is the night of the week when she plays a hand of quadrille with her friends and she could not break her word. So off she went. I took her there myself and will call for her later."

"Where did she go?"

"Calcutta Buildings, it is down by the river. A large block, and I left her at the archway."

"And her friends?"

"Miss Dalley and her sister Mrs Green, they kept the school in the Beech House before they retired." He seemed anxious to reassure them that he had looked after his mother. "We are very busy now so I could not join the party." He looked behind him as if anxious to get back to his work.

The Major said: "We will just walk towards Calcutta Buildings. A pleasant place to live, I believe."

Denny did not answer. Then he said: "I thought the young man did not look so well himself."

"A little flushed, perhaps."

"He has the pink spot, the rash." Denny sounded certain.

The Major did not answer because he was staring into the archway of Calcutta Buildings. "A person is sitting there at the end."

Denny was already marching forward.

The figure was leaning against the wall, a small lady with her skirt neatly arranged about her and her hands folded in her lap.

She might have been asleep except for the blood dripping, dripping from the great tear in her throat.

A sigh came from her as the two men stared.

"God be praised, she is not dead," said Denny.

Mearns was silent for a moment. "Go off to tell Miss Burney on no account to go out into the town alone. Or even with another woman... I will deal with this." And over his shoulder as bent over the bleeding woman. "And if you can lay hands on Tossy, tell him I want him. If anyone can find the King, he can."

Mindy was sewing some lace which had got torn when Denny banged on the door. She put down the collar to let him in.

"What is this?" she could tell from his face that this was urgent.

"Is Miss Burney with you?"

"No," said Mindy laconically.

"Do you know where? Is she alone?"

Mindy did know where Miss Burney was. She had read the note left on Miss Burney's desk as was her habit.

"I do know."

"Where is it? Is she alone?"

"Why should I tell you?"

Denny told her briefly and without details that there had been another attack, the victim might survive, and it was his belief and the Major's also, that Fanny was at risk.

"You too, perhaps."

Mindy did not pale, she had faced dangers before in her time of growing up so close to the gutters before Dr Burney took her in. Her mistress however was a different matter: so innocent, so bold, so full of the desire to help.

"She has gone to Addey's Close to visit a woman in labour."

Denny nodded. "She should never have been allowed to go on her own." He moved to the door. "I am off to the Close. I know the place." And did not relish what he knew.

"Miss Burney is her own mistress." Mindy was already throwing on her cloak. "But if you go, then I go too."

"I know where Addey's Close is." He had a contact there, an petty pocket thief but good at passing on the gossip, and finding and passing on what was going on in the sub-world of Windsor.

"They have infection there too," said Mindy. "Fool that she is to go there."

"Who is the woman she is visiting?"

"Oh a girl who worked in the Dr Burney's house when my mistress was a child. Miss Burney loved her then in the way children do and she is loyal."

Foolish, foolish girl, thought Denny.

"Ladies are like that." Mindy was philosophical. "The real gentry. It's how they are."

—Some of them, thought Denny, who had his own philosophy. He had experience of some vicious ladies of good birth.

Although it was dark and raining, there were figures lounging about Addey's Close. Silent, watchful, dark figures. One of whom tried to melt away into a deeper darkness.

"There you are, Tossy," cried Sergeant Denny, the sharp eyed. He grabbed the man.

"Why'd ye come here? It's where I live. Private."

—It's where you hide, thought the sergeant, where do you really live? Nowhere.

"The Major wants you."

"For what?"

"He will tell you."

"An' where will I find him," growled Tossy.

Denny did not answer, but walked back to where Mindy stood, listening and taking it all in. You'll find him, Tossy, his comment to himself, you always find what you want.

He did not like Tossy, but knew his use.

"Dr Seaton's up there," called Tossy softly after him, adding even more softly, "with his black bag with 'im," and watched them hurry even more.

That's right, lady, he thought, you hurry. We all know what the doctor's like.

Up the foul and smelly staircase, they ran, with the Sergeant first and Mindy after. There were locks on the doors, hardly much light, but a candle burning in the room by the bed.

Dr Seaton was standing by the bed. There was blood on his hand, blood on the floor, blood on Fanny's cloak which lay on the bed.

But no Fanny.

Mindy threw herself at Dr Seaton. "You've killed her, you killed my mistress."

Seaton tried to extricate himself, his face was hot and sweaty, his hands trembled as he pushed at Mindy.

"I know what you did to her before, She was too innocent. She knows now but will not think on it. But I can and..."

Seaton fell backwards with Mindy still clinging to him, she was kicking with her feet and hitting his face with one hand while the other clawed his hair. She was a street fighter. "Killer, killer," she was shouting.

Denny pulled Mindy off, leaving Seaton half lying, half crouching on the floor. "I did not hurt Miss

Burney... never, never..."

Mindy kicked him. "Where is she?"

"I fondled her, yes, I did that but no more, nothing strong, you understand." The blood on his hands had streaked down his face, he was crying. "She has gone to get something decent to wrap the child in." He pointed to the bed.

On it was a small bundle, wrapped in a torn towel.

"The child was born dead."

Mindy leaned back against Denny, slowly calming. For the first time she took in the silent figure lying on what passed for a bed, eyes wide in a white face.

"Labour is a bloody business," said the doctor, getting to his knees.

Mindy muttered some words of apology to Tansy Gomer. Then she turned to Denny. "We must find Fanny, she did not come to me when I was working in her room."

"How long have you been here?" Denny demanded of Dr Seaton.

The doctor was scrambling to his feet and assembling what dignity he could. "I have been about my medical business in Addey's Close before the sun down and since then giving help to this poor creature here. Miss Burney joined me."

—Then you are not our killer, thought Denny, so better go looking for someone else. The King?

"Stay with this woman yourself or get a neighbour," Denny ordered Dr Seaton. "Miss Minden and I must be off."

"Miss Burney." bleated the doctor.

"If she comes back, keep her here. And safe," said Denny with emphasis. "You understand me?"

Mindy was already running out of the room, and down the staircase. "Kill him, kill him," she was saying to herself. "And I would have done if the Sergeant hadn't been with me."

It was dark, and it was raining, but Mindy was nimble footed and Denny was strong. Both of them knew the quickest way to the Castle and once there the faster route through the corridors and staircases.

"It's so easy to get in here if you know how," panted Mindy as she ran.

—Save your breath, thought Denny, for what we might find when we get there.

Mindy was first into Fanny's room, throwing the door open, and halting on the threshold. "Miss Burney, Miss Burney... Where are you?"

Denny looked over her shoulder.

The room was empty.

"But she has been here," said Mindy, moving round the room. "I can tell." A drawer in the chest had been opened and not closed completely, a soft shawl which had rested on a chair was gone, and a bottle of wine taken from the bureau top.

"Is there any blood?"

Mindy shook her head. "No blood..."she looked at a vase on the desk, it was empty of the roses that had once been there. "But she took some flowers."

Fanny had come from Addey's Close, gone at once to her room, where she had been surprised to see no Mindy. She had gathered up the few things for Tansy's comfort, The flowers were an afterthought. The baby deserved a few flowers. She has seen its pinched little face, which had never known life, and grieved for it.

The more so because its mother had turned her head away and said that it was better so.

Then she left her room to hurry back to Addey's Close. The Castle corridors were not totally dark with candles burning in embrasures at intervals. In between, it was murky indeed. Unconsciously Fanny walked faster through the darker passages. She felt she could feel a windy draught moving behind. She shivered, but the air was always cold in the Castle.

Even as she made to leave the Castle by this passage, so the Sergeant and Mindy were hurrying through another to find her.

She was almost out of the Castle, passing through one of the arches on the lower walk when she heard movement her. She stopped, listened, but all was silent. She hurried on.

Then hands seized her from behind, before she could scream and a dark hood was dropped over her head and she was dragged backwards and down. She could feel the cobbles beneath her.

It was too quick and sudden for her to resist.

She did what she could, writhing and twisting on the ground but strong hands pushed her down.

Then she felt the prick of knife at her throat and a cold pressure turning to hot pain. She was choking inside the hood. It tasted like blood, warm and salty.

This was dying, she thought. But fight, Fanny, fight.

There was movement behind her, next to her, all round her. She tried to kick.

She heard a voice. "Damn you, damn you."

Oh God, she knew that voice. It belonged to Winter Ames.

The hood came off from her head and she was staring into his face. He was saying something, then moving away. A kind of earthquake began behind her.

A knife had incised her throat but she found she could scream. She screamed and screamed.

Die she might, but she would go out making a noise.

Not far away, Mindy stopped, she put her hand on the Sergeant. "That is Miss Burney, I know my mistress's voice."

Perhaps she might live after all, Fanny thought. Someone was wiping the blood from her face.

"I must just put this bandage on your throat, it's not too deep Sergeant Denny says, he knows about wounds from the battles. And he says you're a good healer."

"Winter Ames," croaked Fanny.

"Oh he's all right, he's behind you."

"Winter," said Fanny again.

"Don't talk... I'm surprised you can do, after all that screaming."

Fanny found she was on the floor, still in the archway that led from the Castle. A candle burned on the floor beside her. Carefully, she turned to look behind her. There was Winter Ames leaning against the wall, dabbing his face which was bleeding from a long cut; Sergeant Denny was talking to him.

On the cobbles at their feet was a body, all in black, a skirt and bonnet.

A woman, thought a bemused Fanny. But who?

Then the Sergeant gave a casual kick to the body which rolled over so that Fanny saw the face.

It was the face of James Manston.

SIXTEEN

I saw him leaving the theatre and I tried to follow him, but I lost him." Winter Ames voice was grave.

"He was trying to kill Mrs Eleanor Willis."

Mearns spoke up. "She still lives, thank God, Denny and I got there in time."

"I know, I soon heard what had happened, the word was round the town at once. He was always interested in her. I think she had laughed at him once and not in a way he liked. I knew I must go out and find him if I could. You see I had found his diary, and perhaps he meant me to, because he half wanted the world to know, in which he talked about himself as a revolutionary, a man of freedom, And mentioned names. He mentioned Miss Burney, The theatre and the Castle figured in these murders—poor Susan Sandys. In the diary Manston dwelt on his fantasy world, how he dressed up and slid into the Castle, watching everyone. Half fearful he would be discovered, half wanting to be found out. Lord Fred, I knew it had to be someone familiar with both his worlds." He could see Major Mearns nodding his head. "I waited near the Castle because I thought he might go, must go, for Miss Burney."

"As he did." Major Mearns said: "And you knew him when you saw him?"

"I recognised the clothes he was wearing: they came from the theatre wardrobe: *The Double Widow*, was the play, I think. A comedy, ironical, is it not?"

"And you suspected him of the killings?"

"Only towards the end. I saw his face when the blood was painted in the theatre. He was excited. And who in a better position to carry a bucket around the theatre, and do the job when he chose, only someone who knew the theatre would have left the bucket where he did. It showed knowledge..." Ames shook his head. "I saw him look at Miss Burney so often... He chose his victims, I am sure they were not so arbitrary as we might have thought." As to Lord Frederic, he was worldly enough to know that between two men of their sexual persuasion, death and violence often entered in.

They were all, the Sergeant, Major Mearns, Fanny and Mindy and Winter Ames in Fanny's own rooms which were crowded but comfortable. The men had requested permission to light, which had been granted, so that the air was fragrant with tobacco smoke. Fanny had been treated by Mindy and the Sergeant, both skilled in dealing with wounds and had agreed to drink some brandy which had made her pleasantly calm and sleepy. Mindy would sleep with her that night. She had refused to have Dr Seaton, but she agreed that she would let the Royal physician, Dr Jebb examine her throat. Being used to the ways of the Court, he would ask no awkward questions; she did not wish to talk about what had happened. But she knew, she had always known, a little of what Dr Seaton had done to her, but had also known that there had been no rape. She did not use that word to herself but faced the fact in her mind.

"But how is Tansy... I know the baby is dead."

"Dr Seaton is getting in and paying for a monthly nurse... it is by way of recompense," Mindy looked at Fanny, but said no more. They knew what debt he was paying.

"He is a good doctor."

"But not a good man."

"A sad, muddled man," said Fanny with more sympathy than Mindy deemed necessary. "But at least he saves lives and does not end them. He is one who should not have studied medicine because its usage inflames him and gives him powers he should not have. But he has redeemed himself in this epidemic." She looked at Winter Ames, "I suppose James Manston is mad..." Then she corrected herself. "Was mad, he is dead."

"While I was struggling with him, his own knife went into his chest," said Winter Ames smoothly, as he gave her the lie: "It was an accident."

"What will happen?"

The Major interrupted. "A Royal Castle or palace has what lawyers call a liberty or a franchise. All the right things will be done, but I think I can assure you that all will be well, Mr Ames. The coroner will sit upon the other bodies, of course, but will not enter the liberty of the Castle."

He knew now that James Manston had a tenement in the town, the very one into which he had dragged Fanny. He used it for his pleasures keeping knives and whips and old clothes there. Also, where he hung a skeleton, female, and kept a skull.

"Where is he now? Where is his body?" It was a question to which she must have the answer, or she would see him for ever, walking beside her.

"There is a mortuary in the Castle. With a Watcher to care for the body." He was convinced that Manston had had an accomplice in the Castle who had helped him secrete the body in the Castle room, and who had let him in to follow Fanny and to decorate the walls with blood. Who had helped him with Dookey's Nook. That fellow existed but never been identified so far. More work, he thought.

He found himself remembering his visit to the mortuary when he had asked the Watcher to raise the white linen covering the body. Then he had held the hank of hair which Lord Frederic had torn away, held it up to see if matched. It did not, Manston's own hair was going grey and thinning, "From a wig, of course. We must find that wig."

"It's not from Mr Manston?" said the Watcher, the usual one, it was not a job everyone wanted. "You see what his hair is like. No beauty, dead, is he? Death shows up your secrets soon enough."

He had nodded, watching as she rolled back the shroud down the legs, until he could see the small appendage that hung between his thighs.

"He was born so, I dessay," said the Watcher . "He'd never do anything much with that... It would be why he did the killings. Instead of."

Probably right, he had thought.

Mindy stood up. "Gentlemen, Miss Burney is tired. You should make your farewells." Mindy was pleased with the way she put that, she was learning the manners of the fashionable world well.

Major Mearns, Sergeant Denny, and Winter Ames rose. One after another they bowed. Winter advanced to Fanny and took her hand and bowed again.

"Thank you, sir, I think you saved my life."

He bowed again wordlessly.

"I believe I shall take your advice and go back to London." Away from this royal city where infection spread so quickly, and where she had seen the broken, bloody, murdered bodies of young women.

"I too may find my Windsor days over. I may go back to Philadelphia. I have learnt a lot while here."

As he went out, following the Major and Sergeant Denny, he met Mindy's eyes and she smiled at him.

There are smiles and smiles, this was not one to forget.

Before she closed the door behind them, Mindy said: "And the King? What about his Majesty?"

The Major was casual: "Oh, my informant, my good drunken Tossy told me; it appears His Majesty goes to visit, sometimes disporting himself on the way as one must admit, a lady in the town, a Mrs Barty. She worked in the nursery and he has been devoted ever since... He goes there regularly. It is the sort of things King do," said the Major carefully, then he added in a soft undertone. "There might even be a daughter."

After this, having shaken Winter Ames warmly by the hand, the Major and Denny made their way to the Major's room where they refreshed themselves with a drink of good brandy.

"I shall go to London tomorrow," said the Major. "To report to Mr Pitt." He knew from experience that it was vital to get one's story in before it was reported by another. And he was not proud of his work in this affair: too many murders and he should have known about the King's beddings with his old nurse.

"To Mr Pitt himself?"

Mearns bowed his head over his drink. "A very short meeting." But he knew that he was one of the very few men who was able to speak to William Pitt face to face. It was a mark of the respect in which he was held, and the value that was set on his work.

"I shall call on Miss Burney, I heard her say she would be leaving Windsor after what she has gone through." He did not mention Mindy but she was in his thoughts. Where Miss Burney went, did Charlotte Minden have to go?

"She won't get away from the Queen as easily as that." was the Major's response. "I know the ways of the Court and so do you. We shall have her with us for a year more, I swear. And Mr Winter too. If she stays, then he will be glad to be here. Or is it Miss Mindy he has his eye on? Or both?" And the Major laughed. "I declare I never know myself which young woman is more pleasing."

The Sergeant did not commit himself. He liked and respected the Major but to give him knowledge was to give him a weapon.

"Eat with me tomorrow," ordered the Major. "Nothing much, I will order up a grouse or two from the kitchens with some red wine, that and a pudding will do us."

The Major returned somewhat late on the next evening, cheerful and ready for his grouse and pint or so of Burgundy.

He had ridden all the way at speed, changing his horse in Whitehall for the ride back. He was tired and thirsty.

He expressed his fatigue to Denny who also took some wine and expressed the opinion that life would be quieter for a while in Windsor and the Castle now the killer had been caught.

"Perhaps not," said Mearns, savouring a mouthful of grouse. "One of the reasons Mr Pitt wished to speak to me was to tell me that a person of high rank is joining the Court at Windsor, in the Queen's household, and this is a person who is believed to have killed twice already. By poison." He frowned. There was more, even more alarming to the servant of the Prime Minister. But this he would not yet tell the Sergeant. All in good time.

There would be work to be done.

Denny thought about what he had heard. "A dangerous man."

"Did I say man?" said the Major smoothly.